TRAPHOUSE KING 3

Hood Rich

Lock Down Publications and Ca$h
Presents

TRAPHOUSE KING 3
A Novel by *Hood Rich*

Hood Rich

Lock Down Publications
P.O. Box 870494
Mesquite, Tx 75187

Visit our website @
www.lockdownpublications.com

Copyright 2018 by Traphouse King 3

Lock Down Publications
Like our page on Facebook: Lock Down Publications @
www.facebook.com/lockdownpublications.ldp
Cover design and layout by: **Dynasty Cover Me**
Book interior design by: **Shawn Walker**
Edited by: **Sunny Giovanni**

Stay Connected with Us!

Text **LOCKDOWN** to 22828 to stay up-to-date with new releases, sneak peaks, contests and more…
Thank you.

Submission Guideline.

Submit the first three chapters of your completed manuscript to ldpsubmissions@gmail.com, subject line: Your book's title. The manuscript must be in a .doc file and sent as an attachment. Document should be in Times New Roman, double spaced and in size 12 font. Also, provide your synopsis and full contact information. If sending multiple submissions, they must each be in a separate email.

Have a story but no way to send it electronically? You can still submit to LDP/Ca$h Presents. Send in the first three chapters, written or typed, of your completed manuscript to:

LDP: Submissions Dept
Po Box 870494
Mesquite, Tx 75187

DO NOT send original manuscript. Must be a duplicate.

Provide your synopsis and a cover letter containing your full contact information.

Thanks for considering LDP and Ca$h Presents.

Acknowledgements

I'd like to take the time to thank my homie, Cash. Thank you for providing me a platform to showcase my talents and skills. It means a lot. I'd also want to give a shout out to our C.O.O Shawn Walker. You are amazing, Queen. Thank you for always going so hard for Lock Down. We appreciate you, Queen.

Dedications

This book is dedicated to my lil' one. Everything Daddy do, he does it with you in mind. I love you with all that I am. Never forget that.

Hood Rich

Chapter 1
~Rich~

I read over the message on my phone again and again in disbelief. It said, they'd just found my baby sister in the alley, deceased. I felt like I couldn't breathe as I leaned against the whip, my heart was beating so fast it caused my vision to become blurry. I squeezed my eyelids shut tightly and took a deep breath. My eyes were misty, and I kept imagining my little sister's beautiful face.

How could she be dead? Who could have done this? She was just a teenager. All those thoughts roamed through my mind. Macho stopped in his tracks and jogged back to the whip I was leaned up against.

He placed his hand on my shoulder, as I stood hunched over out of breath. "What's good, big homie?" He looked me up and down, with concerned eyes.

I tried my best to control my breathing. I needed my heart to stop beating so fast. It felt like it was being squeezed inside my chest. I took a deep breath and blew it out slowly. I handed him my phone, so he could read the same message, I'd read. Porky and Paper made their way back over to us.

"Aww, hell naw. When you find this out?" Macho handed the phone to, Paper.

Paper looked it over. His eyes got buck, then he shook his head. "Damn, Bruh, I'm sorry to hear that." He grabbed me into his embrace and wrapped his arms around me. "Nigga, I'm down to do whatever you wanna do after we hit this lick. I can only imagine what's going through your brain, right now." He looked both ways into the dark night and handed the phone to Porky.

Porky read over the message and lowered his head shaking it. "That's your sister, right?"

I crouched down on one knee, looking up at him, nodding my head. "Yeah, that's my first sister. The first female outside of my mother, I'd learned to love. This shit hurt, bruh." My heart felt like it was getting worst. I could not believe my little sister was dead.

I couldn't even imagine who'd done it to her, or why. I kept on seeing what had taken place between us the last night we were physically together. We argued over her disrespect and drug usage. I wounded up spanking her. She left the house directly after, before leaving she vowed to never come back and hadn't.

Paper grabbed my hand and helped me to my feet. "Look, bruh, we gon' handle that bitness wit' her, but first we gotta take care of what we came here for tonight. It's too much at stake. Now, I'm sorry to hear about what happened to lil' sis, but we gotta focus on the task at hand. Ain't no way around it."

I looked him over for a long time in silence. His eyes lowered into slits and peered into mine. Images of my sister Keyonna continued to play over and over in my mind. I imagined her lying in an alley, twisted, left there in the cold. I felt responsible. I felt like I should have done so many things different. But the most important thing was that I should have never allowed her to leave the house the night that she did. I should have tried harder to keep her there. I should have tried to talk some sense into her. Now, because I hadn't, she was dead. It was all my fault.

"Yeah, a'ight, Paper. Let's just handle this bitness, then we can jump on this other situation with, Keyonna. That sounds good to you?"

Paper nodded. "Hell, yeah, let's get it." He patted me on the back before jogging toward our destination.

Macho tapped me on the shoulder, and looked into my eyes, before following behind Paper.

Porky handed me back my phone, "Bruh, you already know, we gon' knock some heads off over this. The Misfits got you, big homie. Let's just handle this lil' bitness. You know how the game go."

I agreed, and a few minutes later, with a heavy heart. I stood behind, Paper as he opened the big cellars wooden door after Porky had clipped the Master Lock with bolt cutters. As soon as the cellar was opened, Macho disappeared inside, with Porky following close behind him, then Paper and then me. I closed the wooden doors back and made my way down the stairs that led into the basement of the house, holding my .40 Glock in hand. The staircase smelled like a bunch of wet mop heads. It felt cool, yet damp. The stairs were concrete, along with the walls on each side of us. I stayed close behind, Paper. I had tough time not allowing thoughts of Keyonna invade my mind. I wanted to throw up. My sister was too young for me to bury. *Fuck.*

Macho and Porky were about ten feet in front of me. As we approached the bottom of the stairs, Macho ran ahead into the basement. There were two quick flashes from his silenced Glock. He turned around and waved for me and Paper to follow him. When I got inside the basement, I saw the two big bodyguards lying on the floor in a puddle of blood that pooled around their heads. I stepped over them and made my way to the front of the pack. I tried to remember how my father had explained the breakdown of the house. He'd said that after we killed the two bodyguards, there was going to be another one at the top of the stairwell.

As we traveled through the basement, I got to the door that led upstairs and into the house. I slowly turned the knob and pulled it open just enough for me to fit my body into the opening. Once in, I made my way up the dark stairs with my gun held tightly in my hands, aiming upward. I stepped onto the first step and tried my best to see if I heard anything unusual, but I did not. I took the second step, and then the third. I didn't realize I was holding my breath until my vision grew hazy. I exhaled with my chest heaving up and down.

Suddenly, the door opened at the very top of the stairs. I could hear classical music coming from inside of the house. The door closed again, and the music disappeared. There was a cough, then I could hear footsteps traveling down the dark hallway of the staircase.

I backed off the three steps and into the basement. Slowly closing the door back and stepping on the side of it. Paper, Porky, and Macho stood frozen. Each armed and standing with their backs along the wall beside the door that led upstairs.

Paper leaned into where he thought my ear was located inside the mask. "What happened, bruh? Why the fuck you back down here?"

I put my finger to my mask, and nudged him away, before pointing at the door. He nodded and placed his back against the wall. His gun aimed at the door. Porky and Macho did the same thing. I waited in anticipation for the door to open. I took three steps back and aimed my gun where I figured the bodyguard's head would be.

"Hey, Tony—Neil? You guys alright down there?" Asked the guard as he made his way down into the basement.

I could hear his steps making their way in our direction. They sounded heavy. I imagined him to be a big man. I bit into my lower lip and aimed my gun as the knob on the door jiggled, and then it swung inward. The bodyguard stuck his head out of the door. As soon as he did, I slammed my .40 Glock to his forehead and grabbed him by the throat.

"Don't move muthafucka." I yanked him off the last stair, wrapped my arm around his thick neck and placed my barrel to his temple.

He dropped his gun on the floor and threw his hands in the air. "Hey, buddy, I'm unarmed. There's no reason to kill me. I'll do whatever you want."

Paper stepped in front of him and put the barrel of his pistol on his lips. "How many people upstairs?"

The guard, a tall, slim, Sicilian, shrugged his shoulders. "I don't know, maybe four or five."

"How many armed guards?" I asked tightening my hold on his neck.

He gagged and arched his back. "Two, they're in the living room behind Don Bertolli. The other man is Paulie. They're all connected. I don't think you wanna rob this house. You'll pay for it later. Trust me."

Paper shook his head. "Oh, yeah, well, we'll see about that." Paper waved me away. I took a step back. He pulled the trigger and blew the guard's brains out of the back of his head. The guard fell to the ground face first. Paper looked down on him with his gun smoking. He stepped over the man's dead body and pulled open the door. "Let's go, y'all. Time is money."

I rushed into the stairwell and took the steps two at a time until I got to the top of the stairs in the dark hallway. Once there I twisted the knob and pushed the door inward just enough to stick my head inside so, I could peek around. The door led into a hallway. I looked to my right and could see two lamps one sitting on each small table. There was a white leather couch that had a suit coat draped over the arm of it. To my left, there were two opened doors down the hallway in that direction. I didn't know what they went too, but they made me nervous.

I turned around and told my crew what I saw. I ordered the Misfits to go to my left, while me and Paper went right. I figured the Don, his bodyguards, and my father would be in that direction and I'd been given strict orders to follow so that the mission was a success.

Porky and Macho tightened the silencers on their guns and got ready to run into the house, while Paper perched beside me, and stuck his head into the doorway, looking both ways as I had. The classical music appeared louder.

He stood up and patted Macho on the back. "Y'all go make sure everything good. We coming in right after y'all."

"Say no more." Macho opened the door, and ran into the house, going left with Porky on his heels.

As soon as they ran inside, I ran into the hallway and kneeled, with my shoulder sliding along the wall, the closer I got to the living room, the louder the music got. When the hallway ended I saw that Don Bertolli, an older man that looked to be in his late sixties, sat at the head of the long table with two beefy, armed bodyguards standing behind him. Across the table was my father. He sat with an opened briefcase filled with money. I aimed and fired my pistol twice.

Boom! Boom!

My bullets slammed into the chest of each guard. They flew backward into the wall and crumbled to their knees.

Don Bertolli stood up and put his hands in the air. "Hey, what's going on here?"

Boom! Boom! Boom! Boom!

Paper popped him once in each shoulder, and in each thigh. The Don crumbled to the floor beside his body-guards. I aimed at my father's chest and popped him twice. Knowing that he was wearing a Kevlar vest, hoping that no harm would come to him.

"This is a stick-up! Tear this muthafucka up. We aren't leaving until we got everything. That's an order!" I hollered.

We spent the next thirty minutes tearing the house apart, while my father curled into a ball in pain. I noted that I didn't see any blood leaking out of him which was a good sign. It let me know none of the bullets had pene-trated him. We made a complete mess of the house, snatched the suitcase that was filled with five hundred thousand in cash, and fled the scene.

I had told Paper to drop me off at Aaliyah's crib, but when I got to her place, there were two squad cars in front of it. I told Paper to keep on rolling while I sent, Aaliyah a text telling her to meet me at the corner.

I grabbed the suitcase full of cash from Macho and jumped out of the whip. "Say, bruh, I gotta see what's good wit' my people. I'll get at y'all in a minute."

Paper gave me a weird look, before nodding his head. "Yeah, a'ight bruh. But, after you get all this shit situated you and I gotta have a long talk, so we can get an understanding. I ain't gon' get into it now, but I'm feeling some type of way."

I didn't have time to dwell on what my nigga was feeling. I needed to see what was good wit' my sister. "Bet, I'll hit you up as soon as I know what it is." I slammed the door and jogged away from the whip as they pulled off.

I had so many things going through my mind, that I couldn't even think straight. Aaliyah met me on the corner about ten minutes later. When she saw me, she turned her jog into a full-on sprint, running and jumping into my arms. "Baby, somebody killed your sister. They killed her and left her in the alley on twenty-sixth and Center Street. I'm so, sorry." She buried her face into my chest and broke into tears.

"Aaliyah, where is Kesha, right now?"

She took a step back and looked up to me. "She's with the police. They've been questioning her and asking if she knows why anyone would do this to you guys' sister. She's having a hard time. I think you should go to her. She could use your comfort." She wrapped her arms around me and laid her head on my chest. "I was so worried about you, Rich."

I kissed her on the forehead and rubbed her back. Two police cars turned onto her street. One of the cruisers stopped and shined its big light on us. I held up my hand to shield my eyes from it.

"Hey, you guys alright over there?" Asked the white officer that drove the car. He shined the light from me, down to, Aaliyah.

I had two .40 Glock pistols on me. A suitcase with five hundred thousand dollars in it, and a bulletproof vest across my chest. I started to get nervous right away. Especially since I hadn't changed clothes after we hit the lick with my father.

Aaliyah nodded. "Yes, we're good officer. Thank you for asking."

He shined the light into my face against. It was so bright that it gave me an instant migraine. I could feel the pain throbbing behind my eyes. "Well, you kids get off the street. It ain't safe out here tonight. Been a lot of shootings. The city's going to hell." He clicked the light off, rolled up his window, and pulled down the street.

I noted he parked across the street from Aaliyah's house, before he and his partner got out, walked up her steps and knocked on the door.

I grabbed her hand, led her around the corner and into the alley behind her block. We stopped on the side of a garage. "Look, Aaliyah, I think Andrea might have something to do with my lil' sister being killed. I just found out she was fucking wit' that nigga, Fax all along. She might be harboring some ill feelings because of what happened with her boyfriend, Maxwell. I don't know for sure, but I'ma get to the bottom of it. However, I can't go and comfort my sister, right now, while all of them police are around. I need you to tell her that I love her and that as soon as they get out of her hair, I'll be there for her. Tell her that I'm sorry, and we're going to get through this. I'll hit her phone later to check in on her. Okay?"

Aaliyah nodded and looked into my eyes as if she were struggling to understand me. Finally, she hugged me again. "Baby, I'm so sorry that you guys have to go through this. If there is anything I can do, please let me know. I'm here for you. Never forget that."

I kissed her on the forehead and held my lips against it for a full minute, then kissed her soft lips, while I held the side of her pretty face. My feelings grew deeper for her every day. Since we'd become part of one another's lives we'd been through one struggle after the next, together. Somehow, someway, we'd managed to pull through thus far. Aaliyah was one of those women that were stronger than most. I needed her around me at this time. The loss of my sister, Keyonna, was set to break me down in ways I didn't know I was ready for. It was because of her murder that my heart became as cold as ice to the world.

I rubbed her pretty face and kissed her lips one last time. "Baby just comfort my sister for me until Twelve leave. Tell her what I told you too, and I'll appreciate you in every single way. That's my word."

She hugged me for a long time, inhaling, and exhaling loudly. When she finally released me, her eyes were misty. "I love you, Rich. I love you with all my heart, and I'll be sure to do everything that you've said. I promise."

I watched her jog down the alley toward the back of her house. I waited until she disappeared into her fence before I bounced. I had to get my mind together. I had to get an understanding with, Paper and the Misfits. Chasity and her harem of women were set to be coming up from, Memphis, so we could get our strip club up and running. I had to touch bases with my father. He'd promised to plug me deep into the underworld, now that we'd hit up one of his closest allies. On top of all of that, I had to find Andrea, and get to the bottom of who'd killed my sister. Until all these things were concluded, I wouldn't be able to get any sleep.

Chapter 2

Keyonna's funeral was held at Mercy Baptist Church, seven days later. It was the church our mother would attend whenever she'd wake up feeling spiritual on Sunday mornings. I sat in the front row with my arm around my little sister, Kesha. Dark tinted Tom Ford shades covered my eyes, but they still didn't stop me from shedding tears. Kesha cried under me and continued to ask why our sister. She buried her face in my chest and cried her heart out. It made me sick to my stomach. I hated seeing my baby sister so weak and vulnerable. I wish I could have done something to take her pain away. I felt like such a loser because I could not.

The choir was made up of twenty male and female members. They were dressed in blue robes, with gold around the collars. They stood behind the Pastor's big chair, and sang a selection in honor of my sister, while the Pastor nodded his head and dabbed at the sweat glistened around his brows. Beneath him, about ten feet away was Keyonna's coffin. It was opened, and from my vintage point, I could see her yellow face, her eyes were closed. She looked as if she had a tinge of blue to her. Her face was fatter than when she was alive. We'd dressed her in a pink and black Ferragamo dress, and had her long curly hair done with a pink and black Ferragamo bow. Her casket was all white, with pink trimmings.

Besides the choir and the Pastor, there were fifty people that had chosen to attend. They sat behind us in the pews, and behind them were the Misfits, and Paper. All were armed and ready to handle bitness if anything out of the ordinary jumped off. Macho and Porky roamed around, looking people over closely, while four members from their crew made sure that the outside of the church was safe and secure.

Aaliyah leaned in and kissed my cheek. She grabbed my hand and made our fingers interlock. "Baby, are you okay?"

I nodded, and rocked, Kesha while she continued to cry into my chest. The longer she did, the angrier it made me. I was ready to kill somebody. I knew that she would never be the same again, and neither would I. I wished I would have killed, Ken and Kendell earlier, perhaps if I had, my sister would've still been alive. After the choir sang a few selections, the pastor got up and said a few kind words on her behalf. Kesha took the pulpit and gave Keyonna's eulogy. She broke down several times, while I rubbed her back and held her up. After she finished, the choir sang another song, while everybody was given the chance to view her body one last time.

We buried her about forty-five minutes later. I watched my sister being lowered into the ground right beside my mother's grave, and it broke my heart to look over and see her plot, knowing that Keyonna's was about to be right next to hers. It was a feeling that I would never forget as long as I live. Two extremely important women in my life were gone, and lost because of my own negligence, I felt.

Paper came and put his arm around my shoulder as I watched, Keyonna's casket being lowered six feet into the ground. He sighed and shook his head. "Bruh, you already know that we about to make a muhfucka pay for this. So, don't even sweat it. I got a few trolls out searching for, Andrea, as we speak. Put fifty gees on her head. You know it ain't gon' be long before somebody cash in on that. I made a decree that we want her alive, too. I figured you'd want to enjoy that kill after you find out what's good." He attempted to laugh, then cleared his throat.

"Until, then, I say we get back to the money. Your pops about to put us in. Our traps jumping harder than ever, and I got some shit up my sleeve that's gon' really make 'em hit harder. The Misfits say they need our ear as well. Say they got a lick they want to pull, but they need our approval before they go ahead with it. I love them lil' niggas. I've never seen such loyalty before." He patted my back and squeezed my trap between my neck and shoulder.

Tears ran down my cheeks and dripped off my goatee as I watched my sister's casket hit the bottom of the six-foot grave. Thunder rumbled in the sky, and I could smell the rain developing. I was going to miss her until my last breath. I wish I'd done more. Felt like the worst protector ever. I sighed out loud, and shook my head, as I watched most of the people from the church, throw roses into her grave before walking away from it.

Aaliyah held Kesha in her arms. She and I made eye contact, and she mouthed the words, "I got you." While she rubbed my sister's back.

"I'm ready to roll, Paper. Let's get back to the money until we find that bitch. But, as soon as we do everything stops while I cut that bitch into a hundred pieces. You understand that?"

I continued to look into my sister's grave as the rain began to drizzle out of the clouds. Paper stepped to Keyonna's grave and dropped a white rose into it.

He lowered himself to one knee and said a quick prayer, before standing up and embracing me. "That sound good, bruh. I mean, we still need to holler. So, we can get some things in order, but for the most part, we got an understanding, and that's what's important."

* * *

After the small get together me, Aaliyah, and Kesha made it back to Aaliyah's house at about eight o'clock that night. I'd been holding, Kesha the entire time. She'd refused to eat, and tried to drink a lil' juice, but couldn't hold it on her stomach. When we got to Aaliyah's crib, I made her take a few capsules of Melatonin, then she passed out, and finally fell asleep in Aaliyah's upstairs guest room. My brain was spinning so bad, I just needed to get the funeral off me, so I went and took a nice hot shower, while I allowed my mind to relax, and center itself.

I wasn't in there more than five minutes when Aaliyah knocked on the door, opened it, and stuck her head inside. "Hey, baby, how are you doing in here? Can I get you anything?"

The water crashed into my face. I opened my mouth, gargled it, and spit it into the drain. "You can come in here and wash my back if you want too. I need a lil' tender love and care, right now." I looked out to see Aaliyah step into the bathroom and close the door behind her.

She smiled, and lowered the straps on her pink Prada dress, allowing it to fall to the bathroom floor. She picked it up, and folded it, placing it over the towel rack. She unhooked her bra in the front. Her caramel breasts spilled out of the cups and bounced on her small frame. The nipples covered much of the tit. They were dark brown and erect. Light freckles covered the globes. They made them look sexy, original. She ran her manicured nails down her flat stomach and hooked her thumbs onto the waistband of her lace pink boy shorts that were all up in her crease, exposing the indentation of her thick sex lips. The panties traveled down her thighs before she pulled them from her pretty and small pedicured toes with the French tips. She sucked on her bottom lip, and caressed her pussy lips, opening them, looking me in the eyes.

I pulled the clear shower curtain all the way back and stroked my pipe up and down as I looked over her sexy caramel body. I couldn't wait to get between them thighs. I'd lusted after Aaliyah way before we'd ever laid down together. It was something about her that drove me crazy. "Come on baby."

She placed her pretty foot onto the rim of the tub getting ready to climb into the shower with me. I lowered in front of her and bit into her thick thigh, then ran my tongue along the soft skin that smelled of Vanilla. She arched her back and placed her hand on the top of my deep waves, as I made my way toward her garden.

"I gotta taste this pussy, baby. I need to take my mind off everything. I just wanna eat this pussy. It's all mine." I licked her inner thigh until my nose was right on her pussy lips. She opened them for me, exposing her tiny hole that led to paradise.

"Go ahead, Daddy, eat me. Eat me, right now! I need you," she whimpered.

She ran her hand down my upper back, then brought it back up until it was on my head again. Water popped off my back and neck. I trapped her sexy lips and sucked hard on them, then slid my tongue between her folds, and licked upward hitting her clit. I nipped it with my teeth, then sucked on it as if it was a nipple that I desired milk from. She tasted like Vanilla with a hint of salt. The heat from her kitten was apparent. I dug my nails into her ass and pulled her closer to my face.

"Ooo-daddy. It feels so good. Uh, it's so good. Eat me, baby. Eat me just like that. Fuck," she hissed with her eyes closed and her head tilted back.

I stuck my tongue as far in her as it could go, thumbing her clit while she held her lips open for me. She jerked, and more juices ran out of her. I wet two fingers with her juices and slowly slid them into her asshole. I could feel her ring tighten on them, squeezing for dear life.

"You want some of that don't you baby? Uh-fuck, you want some of that ass, huh?" She humped into my face and shuddered. Her knees bent, as my fingers ran in and out of her back door. "I'm finna cum—I'm finna cum, Rich. Already, aww-shit!" she hollered.

I nipped at her clit with my teeth, sucked it harder and harder, while I fingered as deep as I could into that big ole' booty. I mean Aaliyah was strapped, it was no wonder her body drove me crazy on all levels. I think I even loved the fact, that she used to sell pussy. I was a street nigga, so all that hood shit was appealing to me.

She grabbed the back of my head and forced it into her pussy while she came all over me in loud gasps. She finished and kneeled in front of me. She stroked my dick up and down, smacking her lips together, looking into my eyes with hunger.

"I'ma suck this dick, Daddy. I'ma suck it good, too. I got you." She licked the head, then up and down the big stalk, and finally slurping me into her mouth, and spearing her head into my lap like crazy. She moaned all over it, took it out, and ran it across her face, then deep throated me all over again.

I closed my eyes and gritted my teeth. She seemed to be hitting every one of my pleasure points. She sucked hard on the head, pumped the whole stick up and down, then sucked me for ten minutes straight with no hands, while I stood on my tippy toes with a handful of her hair. My heart pounded in my chest. I felt her nip at the head with her teeth, then her tongue tickled my pee hole, and I was cumming hard like a fountain.

She pumped it up and down as my seed spilled out of me. "Uh-fuck-Aaliyah, baby! Aaliyah-shit—"

She sucked me dry, then pumped the head in her mouth until my dick got back rock hard. She stood up, and placed her hands on the shower wall, tooting her ass up, looking over her shoulder at me.

She placed one foot on the rim of the tub again. "Fuck this pussy from the back, Rich. I want all that pipe in me. Come on, Daddy!" She ran her tongue across her lips and moaned.

I smacked that big ass and watched the cheeks jiggle. I took my big head and ran it up and down her wet slit, as the shower water beaded onto my neck and shoulder. I grabbed her hips and slammed deep into her center. Her warmth enveloped me like a silk glove.

She crashed back into my lap. Her big ass smacked my stomach. It jiggled and shook along with her thick thighs.

"Fuck me, Daddy! Fuck me. Take yo' anger out on me. Yes-yes-yes! Oh, fuck yes!" She grabbed her right breast, and pulled on the nipple, pinching it.

I could feel her walls sucking me as she moved her inner muscles, it felt like heaven. I had to clench my teeth. I'd pull all the way out until my head was just brushing up again her engorged brown lips, then slammed my pipe all the way home, rocking her bottom. She arched her back and shrieked loudly. She lowered her feet into the tub, and bent all the way over, twerking on my pipe.

Her pussy juiced against my driving dick. Her essence along with the shower's water dripped off my balls and ran down my thighs. She reached under herself and spread her pussy lips further apart, running her fingers in quick circles around her clit, while I went to work behind her like a jackhammer, fucking my frustrations away.

"Rich-Rich-Rich, I'm finna cum! Rich, oh, Daddy! I'm finna cum, aww-fuck!" She arched her back once again.

I bit into her throat and grabbed a handful of her hair, then pulled out of her pussy, and forced my dick into that fat ass. Her hole was tight, it barely accepted me, but I refused to be denied.

She was way too strapped for that. "Aww-yeah, this my ass now! It's mine, Aaliyah! Gimme this shit!" I fucked her as hard and as fast as I could, while I watched my dick work, she scrunched her pretty face into a ball.

"You fucking the shit out of me! You fucking the shit out of me, baby!" She slapped at the wall and attempted to hold her right ass cheek apart, while my dick shot in and out of her at full speed. I pinched her clitoris and rammed that ass until I came deep within her bowels. Then I smacked her big booty hard, rubbed all over it.

I carried her from the bathroom thirty minutes later, after we managed to get cleaned. She was completely exhausted and looked as if she ain't have a bit of energy left. I laid her on the big bed, and she curled into a ball, sucking on her thumb. I climbed in behind her and pulled her into my embrace. As we spooned, I kissed the back of her neck, right on her cute little mole, then bit into it, running my tongue up and down it.

"Aaliyah, you know you're my, baby, right?" I rubbed her thick thighs and moved her hair out of the way, so I could see her beautiful face.

She nodded and took her thumb out of her mouth. "I know, Daddy. I love you so, so much already. I'll do anything for you. I hope you really know that." She looked over her shoulder at me. "Do you?"

I pulled her further back into me and kissed her soft cheek. "I believe you, Boo. So, far you been more than one hunnit. You ain't gave me no reason to doubt you." I squeezed her thigh again, loving the feel of it.

"Rich, did you finally kill Ken like you promised, you would?"

I kissed the back of her neck. I could smell her Vanilla scent waft up my nose. "Yeah, Boo, that nigga's deceased. I wish I would have taken care of that situation a lil' earlier. Him and his punk ass son." I flared my nostrils and felt my blood pressure rising.

Ken had been the nigga that forced Aaliyah into prostitution at the tender age of seventeen after her mother sold her to him to right a debt. His son, Kendell I felt was responsible for my sister, Keyonna becoming rebellious and turning her back on the family. Me and my crew had snuffed both niggas. I was proud of that.

"Thank you, baby. Now I feel like I can finally get some sleep. You know I haven't slept eight hours since the day I ran away from him?" She yawned and covered her mouth.

I shook my head and kissed her again. "Naw, I ain't know that, Boo. But, you're good now, I told you, I had you. You wanna lay on my chest?"

She turned on her side, faced me, and pushed me back to the pillows, laying her head on the left side of my chest. She yawned again and covered her mouth. Looking up at me with watery eyes. I kissed her forehead and turned the lamp off. Then situated myself, so I could hold her more firmly, and run my hand down her lower back, cuffing that big booty.

"Daddy, you love that thang don't you?" She giggled and snuggled her face into my chest to get comfortable.

I could hear her nostrils sniffing me, I laughed and closed my eyes. "You already know that's me back there. Don't get shit twisted." I squeezed it and ran my hand into her hot crease. I played with her sex lips, opening them with two fingers, smelling them, then sucking the fingers into my mouth. I loved the way she tasted.

"Daddy, before I'm able to sleep there is one more thing on my mind. I need you to be honest with me, okay?" She raised her head from my chest and looked into my eyes with a worried expression on her face.

I rubbed the side of her face and trailed my finger over her juicy lips. "What's the matter, Boo?"

She sighed. "Okay, I don't want it to ruin our mood or anything, but are you going to be the same way to me even when Chasity moves up here from Memphis. I know you guys have history and all, whereas I am fairly new to your life. The reason I'm asking is because I love you so much already. I don't know what I would do if you switched up on me for another woman. I need you. You should know that by now." She searched my eyes.

Chasity is Paper's sister. She and I were cool, and I had some feelings for her, but I didn't think it was any-thing Aaliyah should've been worried about. She was slowly breaking into my heart. She was like my walking trophy. I shook my head and kissed her lil' forehead. "Nah, Boo, that switching up shit ain't even in me like that. I got a lot of love and respect for you. I see us being together for a long time. Ain't nothing or nobody gon' pull me away from you. That's my word. You hear me?" I looked deep into her eyes and frowned.

She looked into them for a long time, then smiled. "Yeah, I hear you, Daddy. But, most of all, I believe you." She laid her face onto my chest, kissed it, then closed her eyes. "Now hold me, so I can fall asleep in those big muscles. I need it."

I kissed her forehead once again. "I got you, Boo."

Hood Rich

Chapter 3

Paper took his razor blade and chopped through the platter full of cocaine. He separated four thick lines and rolled a hundred-dollar bill into a straw, put one end into his nostril, and tooted a line hard, before doing the same with the other nostril. He pulled on his nose, and sat back in the chair, looking across the table at me with glossy eyes.

"This that shit right here."

I licked my cherry blue wrap closed and lit the tip. Inhaling the Loud smoke deep into my lungs, as I looked him over closely. "Bruh, whatever made you start fucking with that shit like that?"

I was curious because as long as Paper and I had been trapping together, I'd never known him to put shit up his nose. To me, it was mind-boggling. Especially since we'd grown up watching many dope addicts make the transition from tooting to smoking and from smoking to shooting heroin. That was all it took for me to stay away from that shit. Paper tooted up another line. He pulled on his nose and treated his right nostril to the candy.

He grabbed the bottle of Bombay off the table and turned it up. He wiped his mouth with the back of his hand, setting the bottle down. "Man, when my mother got killed, that shit hurt me worse than I actually let on, Rich. I used to cry every single night, and even sometimes while me and you were together." He lowered his head and shook it like he was in deep in thought. "She was all that I had in this world man. Can't nobody duplicate a mother. Then the way shit went down still ain't right with me. I feel like she'd still be alive had we at that nigga Jamie that day. We should have either got him earlier or later. I just wished it never happened, but I can't handle it now, so this is my only escape. Would you believe that I even thought about taking my own life, bruh?" He shook his head and ran some of the powder along his teeth to numb them.

I blew my weed smoke into the air and sighed. "I feel you, bruh. I miss my mother, too, and now Keyonna as well. We just gotta be strong, we can't allow this shit to break us. We have too much at stake and we gotta a lot of people counting on us to make shit happen. You sure, you this shit under control?" I dumped the ashes from the blunt in the ashtray in front of me. They landed on two blunt roaches that were already in there.

Heaven, came out of the back room, dressed in some red lace boy shorts that were so small I could make out each of her pussy lips. Her thighs were fully exposed. She wore a white tank top, that stopped at the top of her stomach. Both nipples were clearly visible. She was barefoot, and her toes looked freshly painted. She was a redbone goddess. Thick as a choke sandwich there was no doubting that.

She walked up behind, Paper and placed both of her hands on his shoulders. "Hey, baby, can I have some?"

He grabbed her by the waist and pulled down into his lap. She grabbed the hundred-dollar bill from him and treated her nose, loudly. The strap to her tank top fell and nearly exposed her right breast all the way to the nipple. I couldn't help but stare because she was that bad. Back in Memphis, I'd turned down a threesome with her and Chasity, a part of me was regretting it just a lil' bit at that moment.

I pulled her strap in place. "Shawty, why don't you take that shit to the back room so, me and the homey can holler for a minute."

Paper nodded his head, and smacked her on the thigh, while she bent over, and cleared a line. She pulled on her nose like he had and when she stood up her camel toe was exposed through her shorts.

"A'ight, but don't forget, I gotta go get my nails done today, Paper. We gotta get me a whip, too, 'cause I don't fuck wit' Ubers or buses. I am worth more than that, right?" She raised her eyebrows and ran her fingers across her teeth.

Paper frowned. "Bitch, if I get up out this chair, on everything I love, I'm gon' stomp you into this muthafucking carpet. Now you heard what my nigga said. Get yo' lil' yellow ass in that backroom, or you ain't getting shit! Go," he pointed.

She scrunched her face and sucked her teeth. "Dang, fuck wrong wit' you?" She left out of the living room with her panties all in her yellow ass. Both cheeks were exposed. Every step she took caused her thighs to jiggle. It was hard to not pay attention to that. I couldn't wait until Chasity got into town, she was slightly more strapped then Heaven.

Paper shook his head and turned up the bottle of Bombay. "Why is it always the bad bitches that are the craziest?" He laughed and cleared his throat. "To answer your question, I do have it under control. We should be more worried about your decision making than anything." He sucked his teeth.

"So, I guess we are getting into this shit, right now, then?" I crushed the blunt in the ashtray and sat back in my seat. "What's on your mind, Paper? Keep that shit uncut, too."

He curled his upper lip and took another long sip from the liquor. "I feel like you getting a lil' soft, bruh.

You give muhfuckas too many chances. You let the enemy live longer than they need too. And you be allowing these bitches to run script on you. I feel like I need to take over the decision making for a while. Or at least have you run shit by me before we move forward or hold back."

I scoffed and rolled my head around on my neck. "That's how you feel, huh? And what brought this on?"

Paper laughed. "The shit with Andrea, Fax, His son. That fuck nigga, Maxwell, and now this club shit with my sister, Chasity. I feel like we should of handled all this shit differently. Had I been in the driver's seat we would have. I just think its time that I lead for a minute and you follow. It ain't gon' be easy, but I did it." He sucked his teeth. "Hated it every step of the way, but I did it, though."

I rubbed my sweaty palm on the legs of my jeans and exhaled slowly. I was irritated, I felt like I was on the verge of exploding. I never could take constructive criticism. That shit just wasn't in me to accept. I wanted to attack him for all his misjudgments and drug usage, but I held my tongue. "My pops about to put us on like never before, and you think I'm finna sit back and allow you to his drive his blessing when this honor is being handed down to me? Bruh, you, done lost yo' rabid ass mind! It ain't happening. I feel like we both made mistakes. We can do this shit together, make sure we stay on the same page. I ain't following no nigga. I'm a born boss, fuck that!" I said harsher than I meant to. I was getting angry and couldn't disguise it.

Paper clenched his jaw more rapidly. He lowered his eyes and nodded his head. "So, it's all good when I'm following yo' ass, but when it's your turn you can't stomach it, huh?" He scoffed and ran his hand over his face. "Yeah, a'ight then." He stood up and began pacing back and forth, and balling and unballing his fists as if he was about to blow. "You about to let this money shit come between us, Rich. I can feel it. Before I let that happen, bruh, I'll let you do your own thing and I'll fall back. I got too much love for you, nigga. Fa real."

I placed the suitcase that was on the side of my foot, on top of the table, and opened it. I took out one hundred and twenty-five thousand dollars that I'd previously separated and stacked it on the table. "Nigga money a never change me. First of all, we ain't got enough of it yet. Secondly, I got too much love and respect for you. just can't follow no nigga. I got this vision in my head that only I can bring into fruition. All you gotta do is trust me, that's all I ask." I slid his money across the table, next to his Bombay. I accidentally knocked the bottle over. Luckily the top was on pretty good. It rolled, and dropped off the table, by Paper's foot.

He picked it up and set it back on the table. "What's all this?" He picked up the stack of hundreds and thumbed through them.

"That's a hundred and twenty-five thousand dollars. It's your split from the lick with my pops. I'ma give two hundred and fifty gees to the Misfits as well. We splitting this pot four ways. That's how it's supposed to go."

Paper frowned and rushed to my side. "Wait a minute. We already pay them weekly. Every lick they hit with us is included in their detail. See, that's the shit I'm talking about, Rich. You about to trash two hundred and thousand for no good reason. They don't get a bonus for coming to work. What are you thinking?" He shook head, then mugged me with seething anger.

He had me thinking I was doing something wrong and making another terrible decision. "Bruh, what's wrong wit' hitting them lil' niggas the way they are supposed to be hit. Long as we're all eating, loyalty will stay amid us. Can't you see that?" I closed the suitcase and picked it up off the table.

Paper shook his head. "Cause that's not how the game go. Just because you're seeing certain numbers don't mean that your workers are supposed to see the same amount. That's how muhfuckas become too big for their britches. After they get their bands all the way up they ain't gon' need to work for us no more. They will become the competition. That's the last thing we need because them lil' niggas are savages to the utmost. They got a group of hungry killers that follow their every lead. All they're missing is money. Long as they ain't got that they'll be dependent on us. It's the reason why every time we hit them wit' a nice amount, I encourage them to go shopping. To buy a whip or spend some money on their crew. I need them to spend them dollars as fast as they get them. The longer they stay blinded by the flash, glitz, and glamour of the game. They longer they will be our slaves in a sense. You feel me?"

I did, it made sense, but part of me didn't like shystying our lil' homies. They have proven to be loyal, and down for the cause, against all odds, I liked that in them and wanted to see them eat like starving fat chicks at a buffet. "So, how much do you advise we break them off wit?"

Paper sucked his teeth and pulled at the hairs of his chin. "I say we give 'em twenty-five thousand a piece. Then take 'em and spend ten on each of them. That way it look like we've done more, but, we wound up saving one hundred and eighty thousand. We can buss that shit down the middle that's an extra ninety bands a piece.

That's how bosses are supposed to do it." He drank from the Bombay and smiled.

I really ain't feel like constantly going over the same thing with him. I opened the suitcase and gave him another fifty gees bringing his total to one hundred and seventy-five thousand. "I'm giving them lil' niggas a hunnit a piece. They deserve it. The only way we going to remain a tight-knit group is if everybody is eating. So, that's how that's gone go. You can say I'm making a stupid decision or whatever, it is what it is."

Paper grabbed the money and shrugged his shoulders. "You'll learn sooner or later. I ain't finna waste my time trying to teach a nigga that think he know it all. I'ma just let that shit come to you when it do. I just hope wisdom don't show up too late. Nah' mean?" He grabbed all his money and turned his back on me, leaving out of the room.

I stood there for the second time in silence. My brain was racing like crazy. I knew that deep in my heart that I to do what was right for the Misfits. I didn't give a fuck what Paper was talking about. I texted them letting them know I'd be on the way to drop their money off.

* * *

When I got there, Macho let me in through the back door. I noted that there were two Misfits in the hallway with ski masks over their faces. I stepped inside, and Macho put the big two by four back over the door. He laid his hand on my shoulder as we made our way up the stairs into his trap. As soon as I crossed the thresh hold I could smell the intoxicating Marijuana. It was heavy in the air. So much so that it boosted the high I already had. We walked into the big den where Porky was laid back with two of the Misfits behind him armed with Tech .9s. They wore masks on their faces. they each had a handgun on their hip, and gloves on their hands. Porky sat in front of a table that was covered with an orange and yellow colored weed. It looked chunky and smelled strong. Up under it was a transparent plastic bag.

He stood up and gave me a half of hug. "What it do, Bossman?" He patted my back and sat back down.

I sat across from him in a leather love seat, Macho took his place beside Porky, grabbed a blunt and set it ablaze.

"It's good to talk wit' shooters in here?" I looked from one of the Misfit shooters to the next.

Porky smiled, his chubby face looked a little red. I could tell he was high as a kite. "We're all a family here, Boss. Secrets are for broken families. Not ours." He handed me the blunt that he had in his left hand. "This shit from Veracruz, Mexico. It's pure, you gon' love it."

I took a pull from the blunt, set the suitcase on my lap and opened it up. "It's two-hundred gees in here. One hunnit for you, Macho, and one for you, Porky. For the lick with my old man. There'll be more to come. Trust me on that."

Porky shook his head. "Naw, Homes, you don't owe us for doing that shit. It's our job, Ese."

"Yeah, bro," Macho added. "You hired us, so we can handle that type of business. I mean don't get me wrong the money looks good, but it's not ours. We don't accept handouts." He pulled off his blunt and inhaled it deeply.

Now I felt like everything, Paper had said was right. I felt like I was making the wrong decision once again. "Look, man, I understand what it is, but this time I want you lil' niggas to eat like we ate. So, you're taking this money, and we'll go from there. I got crazy love for you lil' niggas, and I appreciate your loyalty." I handed the suitcase across the table to Macho.

He opened it on his lap and picked up a ten-thousand-dollar stack. "No bullshit. This is for us, big, Homie?"

I nodded and took a strong pull from my blunt. I was high as a muthafucka. It felt like all kinds of music was playing in my ears. I licked my lips. My mouth was getting dry.

Porky nodded his head. "That's what's up, Homes. And you never gotta worry about our loyalty wavering. It's in our blood, Homes. You and Paper keep us well fed. That shit doesn't go unnoticed." Macho closed the suitcase and set it beside him. "When we find out who did that shit to your sister, you better believe we're going to make their whole family pay the consequences. I'm talking chopping their kids into itty bitty pieces. You'll see. We got the Misfits out scouring the streets using every C.I. we have. In a little while, we'll know what's good. In the meantime, did Paper, tell you we needed to talk to you about this move we wanna buss?"

I shook my head and blew my smoke to the ceiling. "Naw, what's good?"

Porky stood up and grabbed the handle of the suitcase. "Hillside. We wanna take over that hood and have you and Paper flood us with a nice amount of product after we do it. There is a crew of Spanish Flies there right now. They're making seven-hundred thousand dollars a day of heroin and meth. If we can move them around, we can soak up those funds and expand our crew. With the product that you guys have, if we work hard enough we can make nearly a million a day."

Macho, nodded. "Yeah, but it ain't gon' be easy. These Spanish Flies are crazier than any gang I've ever seen before. They are ruthless and believe in dying for their crew, just like us Misfits. Their leader was just killed two days ago, by an Asian crew out in Chicago, so they are trying to pick up the pieces. I say right now is the best time to attack. I wanna hit them before, during and after their leader's funeral. We wanna run their ass out of town and kill as many of them as we have too."

"Yeah, fuck 'em, Homes. The Misfits need to expand. We need that territory. It's a gold mine. What do you think?" Porky asked sitting back down with the suitcase.

"I trust you lil' niggas, I don't know exactly what y'all seeing, but if you're looking to strengthen your mob I support that. I'll do whatever you need me to do."

"Once we take it over, all we need is a plug on the dope. We wanna cover all the bases. I mean, we're good on the weed, but everything else we'll need," Macho said.

"Like I said, I support y'all. I'll even buss my gun for you lil' niggas with no hesitation. Just say when."

Porky laughed. "This crazy, Homes. He's our boss and he's talking about getting down for us. You're a real one, Rich. Sabes Que, you have my heart, Homes." Porky stood up and we embraced.

Me and Macho did the same thing. Afterwards, I sat back for the next two hours while they explained their game plan to takeover Hillside row house. I became intrigued by how their minds worked, and some of the strategies they put together. It had not only opened my eyes a lot, but it also helped me understand that I had to step my game up if I wanted to become the king of my trap. I left out of their headquarters with a new perspective.

Chapter 4

It was mid-August, officially two weeks after we'd buried my sister, Keyonna. The sun was beaming down so hard that every time I wiped away a bead of sweat with my white washcloth, another would appear. Not only was it hot, but it was also humid, with very little wind blowing. I sat on the rocks of the lakefront, while, Kesha stood and skipped a few rocks over the water. She had been quiet, the whole time we'd been there. I was also at a loss for words and didn't know what I was going to say to her. I knew she'd been struggling ever since Keyonna's death and I just wanted to console her as best I could. She kneeled, picked up a small black rock, and skipped it off the grayish water, as a sailboat lingered on in the distance.

"Why are you so quiet, Rich? That ain't like you." She skipped the rock and continue to face forward as it jumped four times and sank into the lake.

I took a swallow from my bottle of water, and shrugged, even though she couldn't see it. "I don't know, lil' sis. I guess I'm just waiting until you feel like you're ready to open your heart to me. I know you're going through some things. I'm here for you." I stood up and walked to her side, tapping her on the shoulder with a Dasani bottled water.

She looked at me with her hazel eyes and smiled. Taking the bottle out of my hand, twisting the cap, and guzzling a nice amount. Then she sighed loudly and shook her head. "I don't know, why we are forced to live the life we have too. I wish things were different, Rich." She handed the bottle back to me.

She kicked at a loose rock with her foot, picked it up, and skipped it across the water.

"Kesha, we ain't gon' have to go through this stuff for too much longer. I'm trying to get things in order, right now so that you can have a better life than the one you're familiar with. You're my heart, and I love you, sis." She picked up another rock, held it in her hand, and frowned, before skipping it across the water. Five Seagulls flew overhead. There wasn't a cloud in the sky. The sun reflected off the waves of the water. The ripples from her skipping seemed to travel about fifty yards before they disappeared.

"I have dreams about you, Rich. Not the good kind either. Dreams that worry me." She shielded her eyes from the sun and looked up at me.

I swallowed and placed my arm around her shoulder. "Dreams aren't real lil' sis. It ain't nothing you should stress yourself out about. You hear me?"

She jerked her shoulder and came from under my embrace. She took two steps forward and squeezed her eyes tightly. Tears fell from her closed eyelids and sailed down her cheeks.

"Somebody is going to kill you like they did Keyonna. I'm going to lose you, Rich. I'm going to be all alone." She fell to her knees and covered her face with her small hands. The bottle of water dropped onto the rocks and fell between the cracks. She rocked back and forth on her knees, sobbing loudly.

I squatted down and wrapped my arms around her. But once again she knocked them away and looked up at me with red eyes and her face wet with tears. "I can't make it in this life without you, Rich. I don't want to be alone. We need to get out of here and fast. Please, you have to listen to me. I know I'm just your baby sister, but

I know what I'm talking about." She blinked away tears and tried to catch her breath.

I grabbed her into my embrace and trapped her in my arms. She tried to wiggle out of them.

"No, let me go, Rich. I need you to listen to me. You never listen to a word I say." She broke out of my arms and climbed higher on the rocks. After getting a safe distance, she sat down, covered her face again, and sobbed into her hands.

I followed her path and sat down beside her. Once again, I place my arm around her shoulders. "Kesha, we can go anywhere you wanna go, lil' sis. Long as you're happy I got your back one hundred percent. Never feel like I don't listen, to you, because I will." I kissed her forehead and held her tighter.

Kesha wiped her face clean. "I wanna go to college, Rich. I want to go to Clark University. It's my dream, and I think you should come down there, too. Even if you don't go to school, you can find some positive things to do. At least you won't be up here anymore. Up here spells a death sentence for us. Our bloodline is cursed. We simply can't make it here." She rubbed the side of my face and sniffed snot back into her red nose.

I smiled. "Man, what would I do in Georgia. All them country boys a try and kill me. I'm high yellow, and from the north. I can imagine what that'll be like." I laughed and rocked from side to side with her. I just wanted to lighten the mood.

I hated to see my lil' sister crying. It felt like I was being stabbed in the heart. I needed to shield her from pain as best I could. She was my heart.

She shook her head. "Oh, I forgot to tell you. I sent those few chapters back to Shawn at Lock Down

Publications, and she loves it, Rich. She spoke with the CEO Ca$h, and he wants her to sign you to a contract. That could be your calling right there. You have so much to write about. What if you were meant to be an author? She squinted her eyes from the sun. Ever since Keyonna had passed away I'd been unable to get a good night's sleep. I'd taken to writing a few paragraphs a day in my book. Every time I finished I'd email them to my sister. She went over them and put them into the proper format.

She'd always been the one pushing me to pursue a writing career. She swore up and down that I had talent. I just felt like, I was writing down the things I saw around me. I didn't know how to write fiction.

"Sis, like I said before, I'm willing to do anything that's going to make you happy. If you truly feel that I should pursue this writing thing, then I will. But I'm going to need your help. You have to keep me focused and on point." I moved her long hair from her face and kissed her cheek, after wiping away sweat from her brow.

She nodded. "I got you, Rich. You just keep on writing and sending it to me. I'll put it together, and we'll go from there. I know that God has more planned for you than the ghetto. We just gotta keep on fighting." She kissed my cheek and hugged me tightly.

That night, I stayed up and wrote three chapters while, Aaliyah, tossed and turned in the bed beside me. I wrote about me and Paper's childhood. When my mother died from an overdose. When Paper's mother got killed. Everything that had taken place in my life, I began to type it into my laptop. After I finished for the night I felt free and relieved. I knew that I was going to be writing every single day. It would become my oasis from the ghetto.

* * *

I met up with my father a week later at the Hyatt Regency Hotel downtown. He'd booked a penthouse suite. When he opened the door to the room he didn't have a shirt on. I saw that he was still bandaged up pretty good. He wore gun holsters, filled with .9 millimeters. He extended his hand and shook mine before pulling me in.

I closed the door behind me. "What's good, Pop?"

He ran his fingers through his jet black, wavy hair, and smiled. Then he picked up a bottle of whiskey and poured himself a glass. "I don't suppose, you drink this stuff?" He held the bottle up and attempted to grab another glass for me.

I held up a hand to stop him. "Nah', that's for you white dudes." I joked.

I sat down on the big bed, grabbed the remote and turned on the big smart screen television. Muting it. "Seriously, what's the matter?"

He swallowed the liquor and closed his eyes. "Son, why didn't you tell me about your sister, Keyonna? I could have saved her." He swallowed and shook his head and set the glass on the mini bar, then he faced me.

I lowered my head. "I don't know, Pop. I know, I could of came to you about it, but I guess I figured, I could handle it on my own. You know be independent like you are. I didn't think things would get that bad. I screwed up."

He sat beside me and lowered his head, as he wiped tears from his eyes. "Son, I know you guys think I didn't love you because I split from your mother and married an Italian woman. But that's not the case. I did what I had to do to gain the power that I have now. I never meant to make you kids, nor your mother feels neglected you. Now that I've had to find out both your mother and our first daughter is deceased, it's killing me, son. I am at a loss for words." He pinched the bridge of his nose and held it.

I imagined to keep from crying. I felt a lump in my throat. I didn't want to experience those feelings of loss and despair at that time. I needed to train my mind on something positive. I patted him on the back.

"They are both in a better place now. We must move on with our lives and make better decisions in the future. I can't allow us to dwell here, because I am not stronger enough to go through those emotions a second time. Kesha is still alive and well, she is my priority now. I gotta make sure that she gets to college safe and sound. She wants to attend Clark University. I'ma make sure she's able to."

My father stood up and wiped his mouth, he looked down on

Me, and nodded his head. "I'm the acting Don for the Bertolli family now son. Don Bertolli is laid up in the hospital struggling to recover from his injuries. After the attack, I took it upon myself to carry him on my back out of the house. I drove him to the hospital just in time. He says that I saved his life. So, does the other seven major crime families. I'ma hero, it's all thanks to you, and your men." He poured himself another shot of Whiskey.

I stood up and put my hand on his shoulder. "Pop, that sounds like a good thing. Why are you so down?" I looked him over closely. I was getting bad vibes from him.

He shook his head. "Just missing, Keyonna, that's all. Wish I could have saved her. She was my baby." He sniffled and exhaled, before taking the shot.

I understood. I slapped my hand on his shoulder and walked away. "So, what does this mean, Pop? Now that you are the acting, Don."

He smiled. "It means that we have the power. Whatever it is you're trying to do out there, I'm going to back and make sure you prevail. Long as you come to me with a precise game plan. I will see to it that your dreams come true. There is only one thing that I ask, son."

I held my chin in my hand. "What's that?"

He sighed, then ran his fingers through his hair again. "I want you to allow me to take, Kesha, fully under my wing. Let me put her in school. I'll pay for her college and set her up. She won't ever have to worry about anything from here on out."

He looked into my eyes and lowered his. "What do you say?"

I felt myself getting heated. I felt like he was trying to insinuate that I didn't know how to take care of my little sister. Or that, because of what took place with Keyonna. Kesha was going to suffer the same fate. I felt offended. Kesha was all I had left. I knew that I wouldn't fail her. She deserved the best and I wanted to be the one that made sure she got it. Not him.

I scrunched my face probably more than I should have, but I didn't care at that moment. "Pop, every last one of them people in your circle are racist. They don't even like Black people."

"Richard, don't start with that again. Her color will not stop me from giving her all that she needs in life. I am the Don of the Bertolli, family now. I look forward to changing a bunch of things. But no one is going to keep me from providing for my daughter." He frowned, cracked his knuckles, and stood up to pour another drink.

I lowered my head, then looked up at him. "Why don't you just say it. Just say that you don't think I can take care of her. That you think something bad is going to happen to her because of me."

He took the shot, set the glass on the counter, and shrugged his shoulder. "Maybe, but that's not the only reason, I'd like to step in. I've-missed a huge chunk of you kid's lives. I should have been there. I dropped the ball. This is my way of making amends. Don't take this away from me."

I exhaled and tried to calm down. I mean it really wasn't my right to gamble with my sister's life. I knew, my father was a well-connected man. If there was anybody who could get her into Clark University, and make it so she didn't have a bunch of debts and obligations, it was him. I was in the streets. I was beefing with all types of different niggas. Some who I didn't even remember.

I was selling crack, meth, and heroin, kicking in doors, murdering niggas, and now I was going to be bussing major moves for my old man. There really wasn't any room for, Kesha to be around me. Her safest bet was to move to Georgia and chase her dreams. I couldn't deny her that. The man in me wouldn't allow it, even though I felt defeated. My father came and placed both of his hands on my shoulders.

He looked into my eyes. I could smell the whiskey on him, and it made my stomach turn. He also had the stench of sweat and well-worn cologne on him. I disliked all the scents.

He frowned. "Rich, I'm not trying to take her away from you. I'm not trying to knock you off your throne either. I know you've been the one taking care of the women of your family for as long as you can remember.

I get that. So, don't think, I'm pulling rank because I'm not. I have a bunch of political connections in the state of Georgia. The dean of admissions at Clark University owes me more than a few favors.

"Also, I've sent all the rest of your half siblings to college. It wouldn't be fair if I didn't extend the same opportunity to Kesha. She'll get a full ride. She'll never have to pay a red cent. Mark my words on that. In the meantime, you'll get deeper and deeper into the game, and build your own Mafia Your connection to me can remain covert. Everything political will be in your favor. I'm working on a few judges as we speak.

"The D.A. is already on our payroll. All it takes is one phone call when you're in a jam, and you'll be sprung. Son, you're about to embark on a journey, you've never thought was possible. Kesha doesn't have to be along for the ride. It's too dangerous."

I looked into his eyes and tried to picture everything he was saying. It seemed so farfetched at this time, but my father had been plugged for what seemed like forever. He'd always been sharply dressed, drove the best cars, dined in the best restaurants, and treated like royalty. His arm in the underworld was strong, and I wanted that same prestige. It was in my DNA to crave it. When I thought about, Kesha. I just wanted her to have the best life she possibly could without the struggles and pain that came along with it. I had to do what was right. If that meant allowing my father to take control of her life until she was able to seek her own independence, then it was what I was willing to do. I owed her exactly that. I removed his hands from my shoulder and turned my back on him.

I sighed loudly and hunched my shoulders inward. I felt defeated. "A'ight, Pops. I guess what you're saying is right. I can't make this about me. I have to do what's best for my little angel. She needs to be as far away from this hell hole as possible. So, I surrender her to your control. Please, keep your word, and make sure that she is well taken care of. It's my only request." I turned around to face him.

He stepped forward and wrapped his arms around me. "You won't regret it son. You have my word on that." He squeezed me into a hug, then took a step back. "As far as you go, I need you to get your crew in order. When you do, let me know what you'll need to get established. I won't micromanage your operation. When you need me, just give me a call."

I left his hotel room with a heavy heart. I thought about what it was going to feel like to no longer have Kesha in the same city as me. Sometimes, when things became mentally exhausting it helped me to be able to go and see my sister so, I could wrap my arms around her small frame. Just holding her brought me back to reality. It let me know why I needed to trap. Her absence was going to kill me. I didn't know, what I would do without her being within driving distance.

* * *

Two days later, my father and I sat her down and brought her up to speed with what we'd discussed. At first, she strongly opposed. But after I spoke from my heart and allowed her to see things from my point of view, she gave in. I promised to visit her all the time. That when I got myself together I would follow her down south. In the meantime, I'd continue to write in my book and send her chapter by chapter. Two weeks later, my pops flew her out in his private Jet. My sister was headed to a new life. It made me feel weak and strong at the same time.

Hood Rich

Chapter 5

In early, September, Jeffrey finally released the four duplexes to me that I'd paid him for. I'd given him five hundred bands for four duplexes and the rights to ten businesses in our community. I wasn't sure how I was going
to handle the businesses just yet. I felt like I had a lot of
learning to do in that field, so for the time being, I simply
accepted the rent from each business owner, while I con-
templated how I was going to handle things with each one
in the future. I turned the duplexes into heroin houses
right away. They were smack dab in the middle of heroin
alley, the perfect location.

I opened them up and served dime sized nickel bags
just to get the party and make the location known in the
area. I made sure that the heroin was barely stepped on. It
had only been hit one time. In fact, it was so pure a few
of the dope fiends had overdosed and had to be brought
back to life by Narcan. Narcan was a drug that was in-
jected into a person who'd overdosed. It reversed the ef-
fects of the heroin in a way that was stifling to me. I made
sure that all my workers had it at the ready. In the trap,
whenever a fiend overdosed because the drug was so
pure, it was like the best form of promotions you could
get, it made fiends travel from all over town to get that
same dope that their counterpart had nearly died fucking
with.

So, every now and then I made sure I had the dope
so pure and uncut that it fucked a few fiends over. My
foiled nickel bags were really the size of ten-dollar hits
that fiends were used to copping in other places I'd pur-
posely made them this fat because I was in the beginning
stages of taking over the new area where the duplexes

were. I recruited all the young hustlers from the area as well. After seeing them playing basketball at the park, looking all dirty and dingy. I offered them jobs and put a few hundred bucks in their pockets right away, so they'd know what it felt like to have a piece of change.

Once they were recruited, I had, Shirley show them how to whip the heroin and foil it up. I made these young hustlers bring their friends and family members to me. Anybody they knew that were around the ages of fourteen to about twenty, that was starving. They came in by the droves, when they did, I put they asses right to work and instilled the fear of God in them through long discussions where we were able to get an understanding amongst ourselves. All I asked for was their loyalty and respect. In turn, I would give them my all with that unconditional trap love. Meaning I would keep it street and keep my word no matter what.

By November, I had twenty hustlers working under me, along with the Misfits. By December the twenty had doubled to forty, and I had copped five more duplexes cheaper than I'd copped them from Jeffrey. Along wit' the heroin, I had them popping the cocaine mixed with Meth that Andrea had invented. It had the fiends going crazy just as they had on our old traps. Money was coming fast and often, at first it was kind of difficult for me to keep up with, until my sister, Kesha, convinced me to take business management classes online. It wasn't long after that I was rocking and rolling at a fast pace. I had to conquer my trap, I didn't know what I wanted to be at that time. I just knew that I wanted to be a Don like my father was.

I wanted to run shit and have a bunch of men and women working under me. I wanted to control my slums, and rebuild them so that they honored me as, king. I felt that with me in control things would flow so much better. Instead, of strong-arming the businesses in my hood by forcing them to pay a certain wage every other week, I used them to help me to wash my dirty money. For every thousand that they turned over for me, I'd give them ten percent. Once the money was in their accounts it would remain there for two months. Then I'd have it wired into my swiss account that my father had set up for me.

Another one of the stipulations was that every month they would have to take part in the monthly picnic I threw for the families in the hood. I'd have the restaurants come together and bring out some of their best dishes to Washington Park. Then me and some of my crew would barbecue for the hood, and pass out school supplies, clothes and shoes. Not that cheap shit either, I made sure my people were happy and smiling. On the fifteenth of every month, in our hood, the restaurants would have to offer each mother a free breakfast, lunch, and dinner. I would, of course, reimburse them, I guess it was my way of showing love to my mother from afar.

I set up a team of older women, that formed a coalition that assisted single women, and struggling families with rent and groceries. We also paid for their children to attend summer programs and camp. As long as it was proven that the mothers were struggling, and trying their best to make ends meet, my group of supportive sistas stepped up to the plate and made sure they were taken care of. I didn't like seeing women struggle in my ghetto, it hurt my heart. I also hated the sight of a dirty kid. I never could stomach that. Out of every hundred thousand that I made at least ten percent was given back to my ghetto, I made sure of that.

Paper once again, wasn't with my game plan. One day, in December I'd shut down and rented out the local boys and girls club that was on Burleigh and Sherman Avenue. Me and my crew took over the big Gymnasium, and downstairs. We were handing out clothes, and school supplies for the children. I was downstairs hooking up about ten, single, struggling mothers with clothes, gift cards, groceries, and even cash if I felt they needed it. I'd brought twenty thousand in cash with me and I was dead set on making sure I didn't leave with a single buck.

It was Christmas time and the traps had been real good to me in the last three months prior, so I wanted to give back a little. It was on my heart to do so. I'd just been handed one of the sistas bills that was standing in front of me with tears in her eyes when Paper showed up high and drunk as a sailor. He bumped a few of the women out of the way all rude like and forced his way to the table where I was and pulled on his nose.

"What's been good my nigga? Why you acting like you ain't fucking wit' me or something?" He curled his lip, and leaned his neck right, then left.

The dark-skinned sista behind him raised her left eyebrow and looked him up and down. "Uh, excuse you, there's a line and it starts behind me. Thank you very much." She attempted to move him out of the way to re-gain her spot.

Paper looked into her face and sucked his teeth. "Bitch, I'll smack the taste out yo mouth if you don't get the fuck out of my face. I ain't soft on you hoes like this nigga, right here."

She lowered her head and took a step back. Picking her two-year-old daughter up and holding her in her arms.

"Look, I'm sorry. He was helping me, though. Can you please hurry up, so I can finish with him?"

Paper sucked his teeth and snickered. "Now hoes wanna fall in line and shit. Just like I thought." He turned his back on her. "Anyway, back to you. What's good?"

I took a gee out of my pocket, all hundred-dollar bills. I took them, and the bill and handed it to the dark-skinned sista. "Here you go, Ma. That should cover this bill and leave you wit' a lil' change to buy something nice for yourself. I appreciate you."

Her mouth dropped open. She covered it with her hand. "But, my bill was only a hundred and sixty dollars. I thank you so much. Can I please give you a hug?" She began to make her way around the table.

Three hittas from my crew closed in on her. I held up a hand to stop them and shook my head. "It's good, come on. I need one, too." I held my arms open for her.

She stepped into my arms and held me tight while her baby remained on her hip. "Thank you so much, Rich. I'll never forget this." She kissed my cheeks and wiped it off with her thumb.

As she started to leave, she kept on looking back over her shoulder at me. She mouthed the words thank you two more times.

"Make sure you get yourself a plate and some of the other things we got going on downstairs. Be safe out there," I hollered.

Paper slammed his hand on the table, looking up at me. "A'ight nigga, that bitch gone. You gon' answer my fucking question now, or what?"

"Bruh, first you need to calm yo' ass down. You can't come in here with your head all up your ass. This is our people. We're being a service to the community, right now. You can either get in line or fall back. I'll holler at you when I'm done serving them." I looked over his shoulder at a heavy set sista that had two kids by her feet.

She had long, weave braids. Her roots were thick and coming undone. I knew right away that I was going to give her enough paper to get her hair done. Her children ran around her feet as if she were a light pole and they were playing ring around the Rosie. She looked stressed out, and on the verge of losing her mind. I felt sympathy for her right away. She handed me her bills, and I began to look them over.

Paper took a step back, wiped his face with his hand, bucked his eyes and jerked his head backward. "Are you fucking kidding me, right now, Rich?"

I saw that all of her bills added up to a lil' more than five hundred dollars. I gave her an even stack, and a two-hundred-dollar gift card. "Sista, make sure you go down-stairs and get the kids some toys. We're also having a raf-fle where five people can win a shopping spree. Make sure you sign up. I got a feeling you might win." I winked at her.

She blushed and lowered her head. "I'll make sure I do that, Rich. Thank you, baby." She grabbed her children's hands and made her way out of the gym.

A red-boned, heavy-set chick stepped forward and handed me her bills. She had a twin stroller with a boy and girl on each side of it. They were sleeping. A four-year-old little boy held her hand, while he played with his Black Panther mask.

"Paper, I ain't ignoring you, bruh, but I gotta do this first. Me and you can sit down and holler in like two hours. That's when we'll be feeding everybody. I would love to hear what's on your heart, man, fa real."

Paper sucked his teeth, nodded his head, and looked down the long line of women. "All these bitches preying on you. I can't believe you saving these hoes." He made a disgusted face, waved off and left the gym.

All the females in the long line mugged him until he disappeared through the doorway. They shook their heads. The gym was noisy from all the children running around. It took me two more hours to make sure that every mother who showed up was taken care of. I wound up coming out of twenty thousand when it was all said and done. If I'd had to spend more I would have. Nothing hurt my soul worse than seeing a woman struggling to make it in the cold-cold world.

* * *

That night, I pulled up to, Paper's crib, and rang the doorbell. His Benz was out front, so I knew he was there. I'd neglected to call first because I knew how his temper was. If he felt, I had snubbed him he was going to act as if he didn't want to fuck wit' me, until he calmed down. By me showing up unannounced it would force him to meet our misunderstanding head on. Behind his Benz, I noted there were four other trucks in his driveway, and two cars in front of his house. I rang the doorbell again. Seconds later, Heaven, answered it wearing a tight, Nine West skirt dress that hugged her curves.

She rolled her eyes and crossed her arms in front of her. "What you want?"

I looked past her shoulder into the house. I had to ignore how she was coming at me or I would have said something real disrespectful to her. After being around all those sistas that day, I just didn't feel like calling her out of her name or bringing her down to size. I was in a serene place. I wanted to stay there, mentally. "Where the homey at? I need to holler at him for a minute."

She sucked her teeth and slapped her hand on her hip. "He don't wanna talk to you. He down there handling bitness with his stick-up kids. I'll tell him you came by." She attempted to close the door, laughing.

I stuck my Jordan in it, pushed it open, and grabbed a handful of her skirt dress, pushing her up against the door. "Bitch, don't think it's sweet because I'm trying my best to overlook your childish ass. You testing my patience, right now. Take yo' ass in there and tell my nigga, I need to holler at him. Hurry the fuck up." I released my hold and stepped all the way into the hallway.

She closed the door behind me, straightened her skirt dress, and locked the door. She was about to walk off when she turned on toes and stepped into my face. Licking my chin. "Damn, Rich. You already know I'm tryna fuck in yo' bitness. Why you be ignoring me so much? It drives me crazy."

I held her out of my face and turned my head. "Shawty, you, bugging. I don't even get down like that. You fucking wit' my nigga. You should have more respect for yourself, and him. Now go and do what the fuck I said." I grabbed her arm and led her in that direction.

"Get the fuck up off of me, Rich!" She yelled yanking her arm away from me. "Paper, don't give no fuck about who I mess wit. He don't care about nobody but himself."

I pointed in the direction of the back of the house. "Shawty, that's between y'all. I ain't fucking wit' you on that level. That's all there is to it."

Paper strolled from the back of the house with two .40 calibers in his hand and a half of mask covering the lower portion of his face. His eyes were bloodshot and glossy. They were wide open. I could tell he was high. "What the fuck going on up here?"

Heaven ran to him, and grabbed his arm, pointing back at me. "That nigga was all over me before you came up here. Grabbing all on my ass and shit. Asking me when I'm gon' let him hit this pussy. He got mad when I told him that it belongs to you, and only you."

Paper looked down on her, then over to me. "Dat,' shit true?"

I scoffed. "Come on now. You know better than that. When have you ever seen me push up on a woman all aggressive and shit? That ain't even in my nature." I mugged, Heaven with hatred, I wanted to slap the taste out of her mouth.

Paper looked me over for a long time. He grabbed Heaven by the throat and threw her into the wall. He slapped her across the face twice, splitting her lip and bussing her nose. "Bitch, you ain't supposed to be opening the door for nobody without consulting me anyway. That's what the fuck I be talking about."

She crawled around on the carpet with blood dripping from her mouth. "I'm sorry, daddy. I didn't mean to disobey your—" Before she could finish, Paper kicked her in the ribs so hard that she wound up on her back. He raised his house shoe and stomped her in the stomach. "Shut up, bitch!"

She curled into a ball, after vomiting all over the carpet. Tears ran down her face and blood dripped out of her nose. Paper kneeled and grabbed a handful of her hair. He balled his fist ready to slam it into her face.

I pulled him up. "Bruh, chill, shawty done had enough. Look at her." I pointed down to her.

She curled into a tighter ball, groaning in pain and holding her stomach. "I'm sorry, Paper, I'm so so sorry."

Paper smacked my hand away and took a step back. He cocked his foot and kicked her in the back so hard that she flipped onto her stomach, screaming in pain. "That's my, bitch. I buy that hoe everything she wants. If I wanna kick the shit out of her I will. Matter fact." He took one of the .40 and cocked it. Before punching her in the face he'd place the other one back into the small of his back. He pressed the barrel of his gun to her forehead. "This bitch is old news anyway. She ain't shit but a pull me down-a hype." He sucked his teeth and looked down on her with anger.

"Paper, come on, bruh. She just a female. You ain't gon' prove shit by killing her. We need to get on to bigger and better thangs. Give her a pass." I pleaded on her ratchet ass behalf.

Paper shook his head. "Naw, bruh. You see, me and you different in that sense. I don't give a fuck about these hoes, and you do. I'm tired of this bitch, pussy. The head is old news, plus I gotta a lil' seventeen-year-old, bitch laying in the weeds. Blame this one on you. You ignored me for a bitch tonight, so she gon' pay the price." He lowered his eyes.

Boom!

Heaven's head jumped one time as it exploded all over the gray carpet. Paper grabbed her by the ankle and drug her into the hallway where he dropped her. "Say, bruh, grab me one of them black plastic hefty bags. I'll be in the bathroom."

I thought he was talking to me, but then five dudes appeared in the hallway with their shirts off. They were heavily tatted. Their eyes were just as red and bloodshot as his. One of them, a short muscular one, brushed past me and snatched Heaven up by the throat. He threw her on his shoulder and carried her into the bathroom. While another one brushed past me with a black garbage and a chainsaw in his hand. I stood there in the hallway frozen for a long time. I was thinking that Paper had officially lost his mind. He'd killed her for no good reason. Then told me that it had been my fault. I was lost and didn't know what to do. I looked over the trail of blood that led to the bathroom and shook my head.

Paper came out of the bathroom with a smile on his face. The chainsaw was revved up. He looked over his shoulder. "Make sure you cut that bitch into fifty pieces. Let that blood run down the drain and keep that water on cold. I'll be back in a minute."

He walked past me and waved me to follow. "Come on, nigga. Me and you need to talk." He pulled his nose as if he was jonesing for a hit.

My mind was spinning like crazy, I bounced off the wall and followed behind him. We wound up in his den, he closed the door, and stepped in my face, looking me in the eyes. He smelled of gunpowder and copper. Traces of, Heaven's blood was sprinkled all over his forehead and cheeks. I looked into his eyes and felt myself getting heated. I was hoping I didn't have to kill my nigga this night.

"You been acting real funny ever since we hit that lick wit' yo' old man. Fuck, you think you better than me or something?" He asked, looking me up and down.

I moved him out of my face. "Nigga, what, cause you just offed a female I'm supposed to feel some type of way? That shit don't hold no weight wit' me nigga." I flared my nostrils.

My heart was pounding in my chest. I didn't understand how me and Paper had got to that point of animosity that fast. But, there we were if I knew any better, I had to be on point. Them drugs were fucking wit' his head, bad at this point. He took a .40 off of his hip and cocked it back.

Then he stepped back into my face. "Nigga, I'll smoke you, right here and right now. You don't know who you playing wit' no more. I ain't the same Paper that you're familiar with. He raised the gun and aimed at my face.

Chapter 6

I looked into the barrel of the gun, then into his eyes. The palms of my hands were sweaty. My heart was pounding so hard, I could feel it in my ears. I clenched and un-clenched my jaws. Sweat appeared on my forehead, sailed down the side of my face and dripped off my chin.

"Paper, you are real high, right now. Now the num-ber one rule of the ghetto is when you pull a gun on a nigga, especially a killer, you better pull the trigger." I took a step forward, grabbed the barrel and pressed it to my forehead. "Bitch, nigga, if you gon' pull the trigger, pull the muthafuckin' trigger, or get it out of my face be-fore I hold this transgression against you."

He cocked the hammer, ripped the half of mask off his face, and threw it to the ground. He grabbed the handle of the gun with two hands. 'You ain't my nigga no more, Rich. The money done changed you. You was my, right hand. I should blow yo' fucking head off." He took a step back and extended his arm.

I was fuming by this point. I was ready for him to pull the trigger because if he didn't, I was going to come back and kill this nigga. There was no way around it, I would not let it slide. Images of him lying in a casket started running through my mind. His face was full of holes from a shotgun blast. I was clenching my jaw so hard it felt like my teeth were going to crack.

He held the gun for about thirty more seconds, then smiled, and dropped it to his side. "I'm just fucking wit' you, nigga. I had to see if you still had that heart, I'm fa-miliar with. You been acting a lil' soft lately. That ain't like you." He put the gun on his waist and pulled his shirt over it.

I cocked back and punched him right in the jaw so hard, he fell over the table and banged his head on the arm of the couch. He struggled to get to his feet before he could I was on his ass. I straddled him and rained down five blows into his face, busting his nose, and mouth. "Fuck, nigga, don't you ever put no muthafucking gun in my face like it's sweet! Nigga, I oughta kill yo' bitch ass." I snapped and backhanded him across the face.

He humped upward and threw me halfway on to the couch. Then jumped up and tackled me over the back of it. We fell on a pile of Jordan shoe boxes, crushing them. He punched me twice in the face, then kneed me in the nuts. That knocked the wind out of me, I hollered out in pain and saw stars.

"This what you wanna do, Rich, huh? A'ight then." He pulled me up by my shirt, scooped me, and dumped me on my back, breaking the tackle in half. It felt like I'd been hit across the back with a two by four. I felt dizzy and was fighting to regain my composure. He punched me square in the mouth and stood up looking down on me.

I felt the blood dripping off my chin. I staggered to my feet and threw my guards in the air. "What's good nigga? Come on this shit ain't over." I kicked the table out of the way and protected my chin as my footing came back to me.

Paper threw his guards up as well. His face was covered in blood. It ran from his nose and dripped out of the corner of his mouth. He ducked his face into his guards and protected his chin the same way I was. "Let's get it, then." He rushed me and swung a haymaker.

I jumped back just as it grazed my cheek, swung a right hook, and connected with his jaw, rattling him. His eyes crossed, and he fell face first into the crumbled table. His legs kicked under him as he struggled to get up but could not. "Bitch as nigga, it ain't over," he gasped.

He slowly made his way to his feet. His knees were weak, he held up his guards, but I could tell he wasn't too confident. "What's good?"

I shook my head. "You don't want no more, bruh. You fucked up, right now, look at you." I jacked on him a part of me wanted to finish his ass off, but I knew nothing good could come from that.

The homie had ego issues just like I did. I was already concerned about how he'd accept the ass-whoopin' he'd just got. It was in my best interest to get out of that crib. I was outnumbered and outgunned. Paper put down his guards. He put three fingers to his mouth and looked down at them. They were coated with his blood. He ran his tongue along his puffy lips and nodded his head.

Then he laughed loudly. "Yeah, you got me tonight, nigga. I'll give you that, but cause, I'm fucked up, though. Wait until my high wear off. We gon' have to go again. You already know how I get down." He licked more of his blood away and smiled.

The door flew open and four of his lil' niggas ran into the room with their guns out. I upped both .45s, aiming them from one to the next. "Call yo' dogs off, Paper. I'll light these niggas up like Christmas trees." I cocked my hammers ready to smoke every one of them, niggas, and Paper if I had to. I was already pissed off and my jaw was killing me. First, Paper had pulled his gun on me, and now his lil' stick up niggas had. This was not my night. They aimed their guns at me and cocked them back. I could tell they were waiting for Paper's word to empty their clips in me. They looked grimy and full of hatred.

A tall skinny one, with long dreads, had two .40 calibers aimed at me, both guns were turned sideways. "What's the word boss. We murking this nigga, or what?" He asked with his face turned into a scowl.

I made up my mind right there, that he was going to be the first nigga I hit up. I had a few bullets in my clip with his name on 'em.

Paper waved them off. "Naw, it's good lil' homies. This my nigga. We just doing a lil' fighting amongst brothers. It ain't no thang. Ain't that right, Rich?"

I had my eyes pinned on his lil' niggas. I was getting bad vibes from them. "Tell these lil' niggas to put them toys away, Paper. I ain't gone say that shit again." I was getting heated.

That murderous feeling was beginning to come over me. Paper scrunched his face and mugged me for a long time. Then his face softened, and he gave them the signal to lower their guns, which they all did, except the tall skinny nigga. The beats of my heart sped up. My mouth got watery, and before I even knew, I was doing it, I'd done it three times.

Boom! Boom! Boom!

The guns jumped in my hand. My bullets flew out of my .45s and slammed into the tall skinny nigga's chest, knocking him over the couch. His guns flew into the air and landed on the carpet beside Paper's foot.

I leveled my guns at the other three. "Bitch, niggas try me. Shit ain't sweet. Next time that fuck nigga a follow orders when they are given." I slowly eased my way out of the doorway.

My guns still pointed at the remaining three. They held their hands in the air with mugs on their ugly faces.

Paper smiled and nodded his head. He looked down at the skinny nigga's body and started to laugh.

"Yeah, a'ight, Rich. You got off on this one, a'ight doe nigga. Whew, this shit gon' be ugly." He shook his head. "Be safe out there, Beloved, be muthafucking safe." He sucked his teeth. "Y'all get that nigga up and take 'em upstairs. He a'ight, he got a vest on."

* * *

That night I couldn't sleep. I looked to my right and saw that Aaliyah was sleeping, so I went into the living room and wrote three chapters in my book. I don't know where the words were coming from, but they flowed so easily. After I finished the chapters, I emailed them to Kesha with a message letting her know, I loved and missed her with all my heart. I was closing the laptop when, Aaliyah appeared in the doorway of the living room with her red, silk, Prada robe wide open, exposing her flat stomach, and supple B cup breasts. Both of her nipples poured through the material, enticing me.

She licked her thick lips and turned her head to the side. "What you down here doing, baby?" She came toward me on her sexy pigeon toes. Her nails were painted red with little Louis Vuitton symbols in them. Her swag was incredible to me.

I yawned and stretched my arms over my head. I'm working on this book, I'm trying to finish, so I can get it to Ca$h and Shawn at Lock Down Publications. They signed me to a three-book deal, so I'm trying to make it happen." I looked her up and down and felt my dick twitch a few times. She looked so good to me. She was thick, and that pussy was fat and juicy.

She bucked her eyes. "I didn't even know, you knew how to write. Thanks for holding that secret from me." She rolled her eyes and straddled my lap. She took the computer out of my hand and set it on the table. "How much money they talking?" She kissed my neck and sucked on it loudly. It sent shivers up and down my spine.

"It's light work, twenty a book, but it ain't all about the money for me. I just wanna try something different. All I know is the streets. I'm trying to soar higher than the slums, you feel me." I gripped that big soft ass and squeezed it.

She reached between us, wrapped her small hand around my pipe, and stroked it up and down. "Hell, yeah I feel you. Now I'm trying to see what it be like." She opened her pussy lips, pulled my dick through my boxer's hole and slid down on it.

Throwing her head back, with her mouth wide open. "Huh-shit, there you go." She arched her back and began to ride me up and down like a cowgirl. She sucked all over my lips while moaning into my mouth.

I gripped that big ass and pulled her forward, so my dick could knock at her walls and started hitting them hard. Her robe slipped off her shoulder. I leaned forward and trapped one of her big acorn-sized nipples with my teeth, then sucked it into my mouth.

"Uh-shit, Rich. Yes, ooo-I'ma ride this dick hard!" She bounced all the way up and slammed down, riding me faster and faster. Her juices leaked into my lap and dripped onto the cushion of the couch. Her walls tugged at me. Her fit was tight, and hot, like a silky fist.

I closed my eyes and helped her move up and down my pole. "This pussy so good, bae. Uh, shit, this pussy so good."

She licked all over my lips, right over the places that Paper had bussed, her nails dug into my back. I could feel them scratching me. She bounced higher and higher while I held that ass.

"I'm finna, cum, Rich! Rich, I'm finna, cum! Aww, fuck-daddy!" She rode me faster and faster. She began to shake and convulse in my lap. I yanked on her hair to expose her neck, biting into it with my teeth and sucking on it like a Vampire. I forced her to take all my dick and loved how it felt hitting the bottom of her hole. I loved that pussy.

"Rich, Rich, aww shit, Rich!" she screamed.

I picked her up, and slammed her back into the wall, sucking on her neck. Her nails dug further into my shoulder blades. I bounced her up and down, digging deep into that pussy. I felt her juices dripping off my balls and running down my thighs. I bent my knees, then straightening them up. I long stroked her walls, as I breathed heavy. It was feeling so good. "This my pussy! This my pussy, Aaliyah! This my pussy! You hear me?"

"Yes, yes, Daddy! Aw-fuck, yes, Daddy! It's yours!" she screamed.

I fell to the floor and pushed her into a ball, long stroking her, slamming that pussy harder and harder. Her grip was driving me crazy. I could feel my head through her stomach. The faces she made were driving me crazy. I didn't know how much longer I could hold back, I arched my back and slammed harder, clapping that gushy, until I tensed up. I felt my orgasm coming from deep within my balls. I gritted my teeth, smashed into her one last time and came hard, squirt after squirt. I jerked and long stroked her kitty until it swallowed every drop. I picked her up from the carpet ten minutes later, after pulling out of her. I carried her to the bedroom and laid her on top of it. Then I slid in behind her, her fat ass molded into my lap.

She lifted her thick thighs, grabbed a hold of my dick head and slid it back into her hole. She scooted back to engulf me.

"Mmm-a," she moaned. "I been missing you all day, Rich. I'm glad you're here right now." She rotated her ass in slow circles.

I licked the back of her neck, then grabbed it with my teeth. I humped forward, slow stroking that pussy, not try-ing to do too much. I just wanted to get tired enough, so I could fall asleep. My mind was racing after what had taken place with, Paper and his crew. I knew there was going to be backlash from it. I had to prepare myself. I was pondering on whether I'd have to snuff, Paper or not. The thought of it broke my heart because we had been through so much together. It seemed like out of nowhere a switch had been flipped. Now I didn't know if I could trust him or what was up his sleeve. It was enough to drive me up the wall. I slowed my pace and left my dick lodged deeply within, Aaliyah. Her walls sucked at me, she reached behind her and scratched my hip.

"Baby, what's the matter?" She sounded out of breath already. She forced my dick deeper into her womb and moaned.

I sighed and rubbed all over that fat ass. "A bunch of bullshit happened tonight. I don't want to get into it too much. I think me and Paper finna fall all the way off. That dope fucking him up." I pulled out of her and laid on my back.

She sat up, grabbed my dick, and licked up and down the stalk. She sucked her juices off me, then took me deep to the back of her throat. She licked all around my head, before swallowing me whole again. She popped me out of her mouth.

"Maybe it's time you move on with your life. Y'all might be headed into two different directions. Some friends are for a season, not for life." As she said this she stroked my dick up and down.

I closed my eyes and humped up into her hand. It felt so good, I was making lil' noises and shit. My toes were curled, and I wanted to be back in her mouth. She had a good tongue game that kept me sprung. Her head was awesome.

"Yeah, boo. You might be right, top me off, though." I grabbed a handful of her hair and guided her back to my pole. She ain't waste no time eating me up like a pro. Her juicy lips slid up and down me. I bucked on the bed and squeezed my eyes tighter.

"I want you to cum in my mouth, daddy. Can you do that for me? I need to taste you so bad. I'm fiending for it." She gobbled me up and began to stab her head in my lap at full speed. Her hands roamed all over my stomach muscles.

My legs were opened wide. I fucked into her mouth, breathing hard, listening to her slurping sounds that were killing me. She nipped at the head with her teeth, sucked on it real hard, then took all of me. That was all I could take. After ten minutes of that, I wrapped both of my ankles over her shoulders, grabbed her hair and came deep down her throat, before falling backward exhausted and out of breath.

She cleaned me up, tightened her fist around my stalk and pumped it upward, milking my semen out of me. Then she swallowed it with no problem. "Mmm-daddy.

That's what I'm talking about." She smacked her lips and crawled up my body, throwing her thick thigh across me. She rested her hot pussy against my hip, oozing her essence.

"Appreciate that, baby. Now I can get some sleep." I closed my eyes and yawned loudly. Through the window, I could see the sun beginning to make its appearance. I had to get at least four hours, or I was gon' be popped later that day.

"I love you, Rich. And thank you for holding me down the way that you do. I know you could be laid up with any other female, right now, but you're not. That's special to me." She kissed my cheek and laid her head on my shoulder like she was accustomed to doing when she wanted to fall out.

"You're my heart, Aaliyah. Coming home to you isn't even a task for me. I gotta keep the grass cut low so I can see all the snakes that are out to bite me. I know you ain't one of 'em." I kissed her forehead.

"That makes me happy to hear, Rich. You know, I would die for you, right?" She rubbed my stomach muscles and trailed her finger over my belly button.

"Yeah, I know, Boo. But, I'd never put you in that position. Hey, before I pass out. You know, Chasity and her girls gon' be up here, Friday. I'ma have to play my role wit' shawty, so we can get this strip club up and running. I don't want you thinking that you aren't my first priority, because you are. I just gotta do what I gotta do to advance us. You understand me?"

"It's gon' kill me. You know how jealous I am. Then she's so fucking bad. Y'all got history. I mean, as long as you keep on reassuring me that I belong to you and that you love me, I should be good. I'm real emotional, and

I've become territorial over you, but I'll be okay. I'll do my best, promise." She straddled me and laid her head on my chest. Wrapping her arm around my neck. "I promise," she whispered.

Hood Rich

Chapter 7

Paper's sister, Chasity, rolled in the following Saturday, at ten o'clock in the morning. I met her at the Greyhound bus with one of her friends named, Poverty. Poverty was high yellow, with green eyes, and strapped like, Chasity. Snow began to fall from the sky, it was about ten degrees outside. The sun was shining but doing very little to bring any form of warmth. I blew air into my gloved hands to try and fight off the cold.

When Chasity stepped off the bus. She scanned the area until she saw me. As soon as she did, she dropped her Gucci bag, and ran to me at full speed, crashing into me.

She jumped into my arms and wrapped her legs around my waist. "Baby, I missed you so much. I swear to God."

I held her for a short time, then set her back on her feet, kissed her lips, then hugged her tight. "You ready to get this money?" I looked into her eyes intently.

She licked her thick lips. She pulled the Gucci skull cap down a little further on her head and nodded. "Hell yeah. I brought one of my girls' wit' me. The other ten a be up here this week. I wanted to make sure everything was in order before they arrived. The contractor told me we ready to open for business, but I can never be too sure, you know?" She looked into my eyes. "You missed me?" She kissed my lips again, moaning into my mouth.

I gripped that fat ass, cuffed it, and stepped forward so that my swipe was up against her front. Her friend walked over with their suitcases and stood at a safe distance.

I tongued, Chasity, down. "Yeah, I did. Why don't you introduce me to your buddy?"

Chasity tapped my chest and broke our embrace. "Oh, Rich, this is, Poverty. Poverty, this is, Rich. He's co-owner of the club. The one I been telling you about." She grabbed Poverty's hand and pulled her over to us. "Don't be shy girl, he don't bite. Rich, she just turned eighteen a weeks ago. But this bitch can dance her ass off. She gon' make us and herself a whole lot of money. The reason I brought her is cause I gotta keep her close. All them clubs in Memphis was ready for her to turn eighteen. But I wasn't going to let that happen, I eating her lil' pussy up too. It's the only way." She ran her finger around her lips.

Poverty bucked her eyes and lowered her head. "Dang, Chasity, you ain't gotta be telling all of my business." She opened her arms and stepped up to me.

I hugged her and kissed her on the neck. She smelled real good, feminine. She had a small waist, and down low looked like a sexual playground. I was hoping I was gon' be able' to keep my distance from her lil' ass, but I didn't think so. I guessed only time would tell. We hopped in my Benz truck and pulled out of the station. Twenty minutes later with the snow coming down full bore, we pulled up to the two-level townhouse that I'd copped for, Chasity, and her girls when they came up. It had five bedrooms, and two and a half bathrooms. A basement, den, and attic. It also had a two-car garage and a driveway. There was a big backyard as well. Chasity ran all over the house like a chicken with its head cut off. Her thick thighs jiggled in the Jordache jeans that cuffed her ass so right. She wore a cut off shirt that showcased her stomach muscles. She'd gained about five pounds since I'd seen her last. She was still small up top, but below the waist, she was hefty. She had that type of body that made a nigga with a lil' dick uncomfortable. I couldn't wait to smash that ass.

She ran up to me and wrapped her arms around my neck. All giddy like. "Baby, I love the house. I love it so so much. Do I own it?" She asked standing on her tippy toes, licking my lips.

I laughed and shook my head. "Naw, not yet. But, the mortgage is good for a year. I handled the utilities too. So, all y'all gotta do is live, and keep it stocked with food. The cable man a be here tomorrow. I was thinking we hit up the furniture store later today. You can fill it however you want. It's all on me. I got you, ma'."

She squealed and hugged me tighter. I looked over her shoulder and me and Poverty made eye contact. Her green eyes peered into mine. I could tell she was impressed and wanted to be down wit' a nigga. She licked her lips and smiled at me. Then she lowered her head all shy like. Chasity took a step back and followed my gaze. She snickered and walked over to, Poverty. Her tight jeans riding into her ass crack. The cheeks jiggled with each step. When she got to Poverty, she grabbed her aggressively, brought their lips together, and tongued her down, while rubbing all over her big ass.

"This what he wanna see, Poverty. Let's put on a show for his ass." She backed her into the wall and helped her out of her tight blouse.

Poverty raised her arms, she pulled Chasity's shirt over her head. Then they stopped and took each other's bras off. "I'll do whatever you say, Chasity. You already know that."

Her breasts spilled out of their cups. They were covered with freckles. The nipples were brownish red. They stood erect like the nipples on a baby bottle. She unbuttoned her Gucci jeans and pulled them down her thick thighs. It was a task. Took a lot of wiggling and force, but finally, they were off. She stood in front of Chasity in a pair of bikini panties that were all up in the seam of her yellow pussy lips. Her labia was on each side of the crotch band. The lips were a golden brown and bald as the day, she'd come into the world.

She ran her fingers through them and looked me in the eyes. "Is he gon' join us too?" She opened her pussy lips and stuck her middle finger up herself, feeding it to, Chasity.

Chasity bent all the way over and spread her legs as she sucked on Poverty's finger. Her jeans slid down her thighs to reveal that she wasn't wearing any panties. Her pussy popped out from the back. Its dark lips heavily engorged. She opened them and exposed her inner pink. Took a cheek and pulled it apart from the other one. Her ass hole winked at me.

"You gotta earn some of his dick, Poverty. He belongs to me. But I guess I can be nice enough to let you see it." She kissed Poverty's pussy and licked up and down the slit. Then Looked over her shoulder at me as Poverty moaned at-the-top of her lungs. "Show her that dick, baby, it's good." She sucked, Poverty's sex lip into her mouth, and placed her thick thigh on her shoulder.

I kneeled in front of her and watched her slip two fingers up her cat, working them in and out at full speed. My pipe was rock hard already. I opened my Moschino's, and pulled that boy out, stroking him up and down. I couldn't take my eyes off how fat, Poverty's pussy was. I found it alluring. I wanted to hit that shit, bad. I walked closer to them, close enough for Poverty to reach out and grab a hold of it, while Chasity sucked first one of her lips, and then the other. She stuck her tongue as far into her as it would go and slurped her juices.

Poverty pumped my pipe and moaned. "Uh, what I gotta do, Chasity. Uh, what I gotta do so he can fuck me with this big ass dick. I want some?" She whimpered, squatting down enough, so, she could feel her mouth better. She rocked back and forth into her mouth, pumping me up and down.

Chasity took her mouth away and kept two fingers stuck all the way up her slit. "First you gotta watch him fuck me. If he still wanna fuck you after he hit this pussy, then it's good. But I don't know if you ready for all of that." She licked her slit again and stood up to face me.

Poverty dropped to her knees in front of me and kissed my dick head then sucked him into her mouth. She popped him out and licked all around him. She jerked him looking up at me. "Please keep this hard after you cum in her. I need you to fuck me, okay?" She ran my head all over her lips.

Somehow, we made it upstairs. I had plans on having Chasity fully furnish the house, so the only thing I'd put in there was a few air mattresses to ensure that she and her girls wouldn't have to sleep on the floor until things were situated. Chasity climbed onto the mattress on all fours. She laid her face on the big pillow and spread her cheeks.

She licked her lips and moaned deep in her throat. "Fuck me as hard as you can, Rich. Just like you always did. I ain't had no dick since you left, Memphis. A bitch's tongue can only do so much for me. I need that meat." She opened her sex lips and closed her eyes.

Poverty slid the condom on to my dick with her mouth. Then she rolled it the rest of the way down with her left hand. "Please remember what I said. I know you a savage, I need some of this." She kissed the head again and slid a finger up herself.

I got behind Chasity, ran my head up and down her wet lips, before crashing into her. My dick forced its way through her tight tunnel. Her ass cheeks jiggled, she, shrieked and slammed back into me. "Mmm, now fuck me hard. Rich, kill this shit. Show this lil' bitch how you get down."

I took a hold of her waist and got to fucking her as hard as I could. I murdered that ass, loving the heat from her insides.

"Huh—huh—uh. Aww, fuck yeah! Yeah, Rich, you—ooo-fuck yeah," she moaned.

Poverty stepped behind me and licked my back. She dropped down and stuck her face between our sex parts. She licked at our juices with her hand between her legs. Her fingers went in and out of her slit. "Y'all smell so good. Ooh, I can't wait til' my turn."

I pulled, Chasity's hair, fucking the shit out of Paper's sister. The thought of who she was to him, made me hit that shit as hard as I could, with no mercy. I tried to pull her tracks out of her scalp.

"Awww, fuck, Rich, stop! Oooh, you killing me! You killing this pussy! You killing it, Rich—yes." She laid her face back onto the air mattress while I tamed that ass.

Poverty climbed on to the bed, sat in front of Chasity, opened her thick thighs wide. She peeled her golden lips apart. "Eat my pussy, Chasity. Eat me, hurry up. I don't just wanna watch y'all fuck until it's my turn," she whimpered pinching her own clit.

Chasity went right to work on her. She crashed back into me at the same time. Poverty looked into my eyes and lowered hers.

She mouthed the words. "I can't wait!"

I pulled all the way back, before banging into, Chasity. Her pussy was wet and leaking. It smelled of cherries. I watched Poverty ride her face. Her pretty titties jiggled on her chest. She squeezed them together, then pulled on her nipples, licking them.

Chasity slammed back into me five hard times. "Here I come, Rich. Uh-shit, I'm coming, boo," she screamed, and humped back ten times in a row, before shuddering all over me.

She fell forward and left my hard dick in the air throbbing like crazy. Poverty rolled her to the side and climbed across her body. She took a hold of my dick and sucked, Chasity's juices from it. She looked me in the eyes, holding him tight.

"I want you to fuck me just as hard as you did her. I can take it, I need this grown dick in my life." She laid on her back and opened her thick thighs. She spread her pussy lip, showing off the groove to her hole. I got between them legs, with Chasity licking all over my neck. She stuck her tongue in my ear and blew into it. I lined my pipe up and tried to force it into, Poverty but it was a tight fit. I noticed she winced and backed away a lil bit.

I frowned, grabbed her hips and pulled her back under me. "What's good wit' her?" I asked, kissing, Chasity on the lips. I could taste, Poverty's pussy on them. The scent went up my nose.

Chasity shook her head. "That girl ain't never had no dick before. I told her that I wanted her first time to be with a savage. She think, she ready, so I want you to break her ass in the right way. I'm telling you she gon' be our cash cow." She stuck her tongue in my ear, and twirled it around, sending shivers all through me.

I dug my nails into, Poverty's thick ass thighs, and pulled her under me, trapping her. I pinched her clitoris, rubbing it in circles. Juices leaked from the top of her slit and oozed out of her hole. "You want this dick, shawty, huh? You want me to break this lil' pussy in for you?"

She slipped a finger into herself. "Hell yeah, please. Just do me like you did, Chasity. I know it gone hurt, but I don't care." She opened her lips wider, and arched her back, and sat up to kiss my lips.

I pushed her lil' ass back down and jerked my head away from Chasity. I lined my head up between her thick, golden lips, and slammed my dick into her tight hole, hitting rock bottom.

"Aww—shit!" She screamed, sitting all the way up, pushing, at my chest.

"Un, un that shit hurt. Wait a minute, let me get used to it." She blinked, and a tear fell from her eyes. She dropped her mouth open and breathed very hard.

Chasity climbed behind her and held her as if she was going to support her in labor. She kissed all over her neck, then they got to making out with long tongues. They kissed and sucked each other's lips, wildly.

"Fuck this bitch, Rich. No mercy her ass. She gon' love you for it in the end, trust me, bae."

Poverty laid back and opened her thighs again. Chasity held her clit and tongued her down some more. I grabbed her to me, slid back in the path I'd already created with my sword and got to fucking her like a champion. I juiced that tight ass pussy, beating down them walls. I honestly didn't know if I was the first nigga to actually hit the pussy. But, what I can say is that pussy was so tight I could barely fit into it. It was steamy, gushy and soft on the insides.

She had these lil' ridges too. I found that odd, but great. I got to fucking her so hard that Chasity backed away from her and started to finger herself. She kept her eyes pinned on my dick slushing in and out of, Poverty's fresh pussy. I was stretching that shit open. Showing her how a real nigga got down with that pussy. She threw her head back and moaned at the top of her lungs.

I knew the neighbors could hear her. It was impossible not to. "He fucking me, Chasity! This grown nigga fucking me! He fucking me so hard! Uh, shit! Uh, fuck, it's so good," she cried with tears rolling down her checks.

She began to shake and make some really crazy sounds. Her tongue licked all over her lips. Her nipples were rock hard. I flipped her onto her stomach, laid on her back, and slid back into her, fucking the shit out of her. I had to feel that big ass booty in my lap. This girl was strapped beyond describing. I long stroked that pussy, landing on her soft cheeks. I held her right thigh in my hand, rolling my back, giving her that good dick. My own eyes were rolling into the back of my head. I whimpered deep in my throat and tried to stop myself from coming, but I could feel it building up like never before.

"Damn, this pussy! This pussy—aww! Poverty, yo' pussy! Shit, aww," I growled, and really got to killing that shit at full speed. The air mattress was sliding across the floor. She was hanging halfway off it, and I kept right on going.

"Shit-shit-shit! Aww, he, killing me—he killing me, Chasity! Chasity!" She screamed, scratching at the hardwood floor while I pummeled that ass.

Chasity reached under us and opened, Poverty's ass. I saw her brown eyes, all crinkled, glistening with sweat, and it was too much. I got to cumming hard and jerking, over and over again. I pulled my dick out of her and saw that the head was sticking through the condom. I'd broken it. I dropped the rest of my semen all over her ass crack. Took the head and forced it into her hole back there. She rose to all fours and laid her face on the mattress.

"Fuck, shawty, you hot back here." Chasity held her ass cheeks opened for me. I cocked back and slammed into her with all my might.

She tried to run, I grabbed a hold of her hair and pulled her back to me. I humped into that juicy booty, it was so fucking fat. I just had too. I wasn't gon' be able to let her walk 'round me strapped like that without tapping that asshole. I had to see what that was like. It was as good as advertised. Chasity, played with her clit, while I fucked her ass harder and harder, and while she forced me to go deeper. This girl was built for sex. I smacked that ass and did my thing, while she bounced off all the meat back there.

"Be gentle, be gentle, Rich! Aww, fuck, you be gentle! Please," she screamed. "Yes, fuck-yes!"

After it was all said and done. We got in the big tub with Chasity sitting in front of me, and Poverty in front of her. The bubble bath smelled of Apricots and Peaches. We'd added three different bath salts and a hint of

Peroxide. I laid back and played between Chasity's legs. Her meaty pussy felt good under my fingers.

"We gotta make this thing happen, baby. I'm gon' allow you to do your thing with this club. I got a few people we're going to meet that can ensure our launching will be a success. People that my pops put me in touch with. So, be ready to have your game face on." I kissed her on the cheek and fed her my fingers.

She sucked them into her mouth. "I got you, Bae. You know I won't squander this opportunity. I got three people here that are going to hold me down. Two of them own clubs in the city already, as well as other places. They are my mothers' connects and feel like they owe her a favor. So, just trust me on this and watch me work. I won't let you down."

* * *

We'd decided to name the club, The Garden of Eden, it took two months for us to get everything situated. In the third month, the club was going hard and kept a full house. Chasity had filled it with top-notch strippers from the south. Females with class, and all about their paper. My father helped me with the promotions, and to get it on the map. Chasity also used her connects that did everything they could to help us to go hard. The end resulted in The Garden of Eden, doing big numbers every Thursday, Friday, and Saturday. We averaged no less than twenty thousand a night. I felt that was a good start, and I had so many more ideas in my head that would bring financial success the legal way. I was starting to want something bigger than the hood. After my chips rose to three million, I was already Hood Rich.

Hood Rich

Chapter 8

Porky rolled down on me, one Friday around the end of March. He was rolling in a black, and gold Porsche, with gold rims, and mirror tinted windows. I knew it was him because the license plates read his nickname, Porky. I'd copped a two-level, red-bricked, house out in Wauwatosa. An upper middle class predominantly white neighborhood that mostly had doctors, lawyers, and white-collar people of that upper class. I had my red BMW in the driveway, spraying it down with a water hose after giving it a nice wash and shine.

Aaliyah was on her way out of the house, with a picture of fresh squeezed lemonade, when he showed up. I waved her back into the house. Not that I was worried about anything. I just knew we were about to talk business and I didn't want her eavesdropping. I made it my business to keep her as far away from the street life as possible. She was finishing business, and cosmetology courses at this point. We were already working on opening her a salon, and nail shop. I wanted her to strive higher than the ghetto. She deserved that. So, I had to make it happen.

I turned off the water hose. Porky walked up to me and gave me a half hug, patting my back. "What's good, Bossman?"

I shook my head. "Just living life for a minute, bruh. What's good wit' you?"

I didn't make it a habit of letting people know where I laid my head because I had done so much in the streets. But it was something about, Porky and Macho, that made trust them. They had never given me reason not too and that's saying a lot. Cause I didn't trust nobody, not even my reflection in the mirror.

Porky, smiled, then turned it into a scowl. "We found that bitch, Andrea. Got her down in the dungeon tied up and waiting for your presence. Bitch been trying to explain herself the whole time. Until I put duct tape across her mouth. I don't wanna hear that shit. I know the situation with her is close to your heart, so we decided to let you handle it."

A chubby, Robin, landed on the hood of my BMW. Before I could shoo it away, Porky, waved his hands at it. It flew into the sky, then up into a tree. The sun shined down on my forehead. I got to imagining, Keyonna, and her face. I felt the anger all over again. I knew Andrea was mildly responsible for her death.

I nodded and hugged the homie. "I'll be out there tonight, lil bruh. Keep shawty where she is. I appreciate this too."

He smiled. "That's cool, but you gon' have to come through before seven. We gotta make our last round on these Spanish Flies. It's only a few left in Hillside. One lil' sweep tonight, and that hood officially belongs to the Misfits."

He shook up with me and nodded his head. "I'm holler later. Gon' do your thing. I'ma tell, Macho, what it is." He pulled out a Newport and lit the tip. Got in his whip and stormed away from the curb.

Aaliyah waited for a few minutes before she came back outside. She wrapped her arm around my lower waist and laid her head on my shoulder. "Everything okay, baby? You seem tense."

I turned on the water hose and directed it away from us. "They just found that bitch, Andrea. Got her down in the dungeon. I can't stop thinking about ways to kill her ass. This bitch took my sister away from me. I'm still hurting like crazy."

"Rich, I'm two months pregnant with our child." She looked up to me after taking a step back.

I frowned and jerked my head back. Birds flew over my head, chirpin' loudly. One of the neighbors turned on his lawnmower. Two white women jogged past our home and waved at us with smiles on their faces. They looked happy.

"When did you find this out, Aaliyah?"

She lowered her head. "I should of known you weren't going to be happy. I don't know what to do," she sighed in defeat.

I shook my head and held her pretty face in my hands. "Aww, naw, baby. It's not that, I'm very very happy. Come here." I grabbed her into my arms and planted kisses all over her face, before picking her up into the air, twirling her around in a circle.

The last thing I wanted to do was make her feel bad about having our kid. I loved this woman. She'd become my rock. I wanted only the best for her, against all odds. She landed on her feet, with a big smile on her face. I kneeled in front of her and kissed her sexy caramel stomach with the light traces of freckles all over it.

"How long have you known, baby?"

"For about three weeks now, I wanted to tell you, but you've had so much going on. I didn't want to burden you with anything else. I know you're doing all that you can to make it happen for us. And I'm not doing much." She exhaled and looked into my eyes again. "I'm sorry, daddy."

I stood up and held her face. "Baby, look at me. You are doing just as much for me as I am for you. You have no idea how much I appreciate you, and that's my fault because I gotta get better at showing you just how much. The fact that you thought I'd be saddened by this news says a lot. So, I apologize, and I promise I'll get better at things, so I can be there for you." I hugged and held her for about two minutes, loving the feel of her in my arms.

She broke our embrace and rubbed the side of my face. "I don't know why, God, blessed me with a good man like you. But I am very thankful. I know that once you leave those streets alone, we're going to have a happy life together. I was talking wit', Kesha on Facebook. She was saying that Atlanta is the place to be. We could move there and start all over. Get away from this city that has brought us so much pain and agony. Raise our family under a new umbrella, in a new setting, you know?"

An older white man walked past with his German Shepherd on a leash. He waved at us and kept right on walking. He had on a big pair of sunglasses. His legs looked sun cooked, and on the verge of peeling. I turned off the water hose and laid it beside the tire of my BMW. Took, Aaliyah's hand and escorted her toward the house. We sat on the porch steps, luckily there was shade from the big tree in my yard to cover us. A nice breeze sailed through.

"Baby, all my money is tied up in this city. It's gon' be at least a year before I'm able to venture anywhere else. I'm not saying it's not in the cards, but it's down the line some."

She lowered her head between her legs. Her thick thighs were exposed by the small, white, Fendi shorts she wore. Her skin was oiled and popping, and she smelled good, too. It was one of the reasons, I was falling for her. For me, there was nothing sexier than a well-kept woman.

Everything stayed tip top on Aaliyah, her hair, nails, and clothes. I couldn't see it any other way.

"Baby, I just got a bad feeling deep in my gut. It's telling me that something bad and devastating is about to happen to us. I don't know what it is, but some nights I stay up, so I can watch you sleep. I put my hand on your chest as it rises and falls. I place my finger under your nostrils to remind me that there is air coming out of your lungs. I don't know what I would do if anything happened to you. You're my everything. I wish we could leave everything behind. Please." She laid her head on my chest and wrapped her arm around my neck.

I could smell her Dove deodorant. I sighed and held her close. "Ever since we've been a part of each other, Aaliyah, your gut has never been wrong." I placed my hand on her stomach and rubbed it in a circular motion. Then I kissed her neck and inhaled her. She smelled so feminine, it was like food to my soul. There was nothing like the essence of a woman. It made life make sense to me. "Baby, let me just go hard for the next three months. Then we'll get out of here. We'll move down to Georgia with, Kesha, get married, and raise our child the right way. I feel like it's time for me to turn over a new leaf, just as much as you do. We're going to be parents. It's time I act like it. I love you, Boo."

She hugged my neck harder and started to whimper. "Are you serious? You're going to marry me?" She looked into my eyes with her big brown ones and a tear dripped down her cheek.

I wiped it away with my thumb and nodded. "It's always been you, Aaliyah. Even when I tried to fight it, and keep it buddy between us, I couldn't. You've always invaded my fantasies. It gotta be you, I love you too much!" I kissed her lips and slid my tongue into her mouth.

She closed her eyes and gave me the most passionate kiss she could. After breaking it, she wiped my lips with her thumb. "Baby, why don't you give Andrea a pass? You ain't gotta kill her, even though, I know it's gone be hard not to. But, I think we should move on with our lives. Just let God get her back, Karma is a bitch. If it's one thing we've learned, it's that."

I took a deep breath and shook my head. "As much sense as you're making, I can't let that shit slide, she took my first sister away from me. I can't honor that, everybody that had something to do with, Keyonna being hurt gotta pay the piper. That's how that has to go. I consider Andrea, unfinished business. I will never be able to sleep until I make her answer for her sins. That's the real." I stood up and scanned the neighborhood.

The two white, jogging women, from before were on their way back pass our house. Once again, they waved at us and kept going. I saluted them, while Aaliyah waved back.

She stood up and hugged me. "Well, I will hold my peace on this. But, in three months I expect to be out of here. We have to start over. All of our sins are here."

"Three months, Boo. We'll be out of here by mid-June. I'ma make it by bitness." I kissed her lips and cuffed that big booty.

* * *

I turned up the bottle of Patron, guzzling like it was water, before handing the bottle back to Porky. "Porky, hold this, bruh."

He handed me the big can of Peanut butter. I walked in front of a tied, Andrea. She sat with her hands behind her body, duct tape around her wrist and ankles and tears streaming down her face.

I felt nothing as I ripped the tape from her mouth. "You ready to talk now?" I growled, scooping out four fingers full of peanut butter.

She shook her head. "Rich, I ain't have shit to do with your sister being killed. You know I wouldn't lay a finger on that girl. I been there for y'all ever since your mother passed away. I love y'all—arrgh!"

I stuffed the glob of peanut butter into her mouth. Then forced it as deep into her mouth as it would go. "Swallow this shit bitch. Swallow it before I have the homey blow yo' muthafucking brains all over this basement." I scooped out an even thicker portion as I watched her struggle to chew and swallow.

She smacked loudly with water running down her cheeks. She shook her head and breathed through her nose loudly. Snot bubbled out of her nostrils. I could hear her wheezing. She extended her neck and tried her best to get the peanut butter down. "I can't breathe, Rich," she gasped.

"Bitch, tell me what happened with my sister. I'm giving you a chance to save your life and you're blowing it. Now tell me!"

She swallowed and coughed, then shook her head, crying. "Rich, I didn't mean too. Fax had me watching over her, and then she said she'd tell you what was good.

I wouldn't let her do that, so—" she stopped and started crying harder, shaking her head from left to right.

"So, what bitch?" I grabbed her hair and force another glob of peanut butter into her mouth and another.

Macho handed me a metal bowl of crushed Saltine crackers. I grabbed a hand full of them, ready to force them into her orifice.

She stomped her tied feet on the ground. Her eyes were bugged out of her head. She coughed, and a huge portion of the peanut butter came out and landed in the lap of her Burberry, cheerleading skirt. "Ack—ack! Fax, made me tie a rope around her neck and kill her. He forced me to. After I told him what she said, he told me to or he was going to kill me. He's crazy," she cried, choking on her spit.

I grabbed her by the throat and leaned into her face. "Bitch, after all, we been through, you had the nerve to kill my baby sister? You took her away from me!" I began to shed tears and lowered my head.

I imagined Keyonna's face, the first time I'd held her when she was a baby. All the times she reached up for me to pick her up as a kid. Then I flashed back to our last argument. I'd spanked her, and she'd stormed out the house, never to return. It had been all my fault. I should of done more, I should have protected my sister and forced her to stay home. Made sure that she was good, but I hadn't. Now she was gone killed by the hands of an overt enemy.

Y'all hold this bitch head for me," I said barely above a whisper.

Macho and Porky took a side and held her head in place. They looked me over closely with understanding

"Please don't do this, Rich. Please, I'm so sorry. I am begging you, please have mercy on me," she pleaded.

I dug out a glob of peanut butter and stuffed it into her mouth again. She tried to spit it out, but I kept stuffing more and more. I dug deeper and got it into her mouth while she cried. Next came the crackers, I shoved at least half of the bowl into her mouth, while she cried. When her cheeks were puffy I slapped the duct tape back over her mouth, pinched her nose and held it hard. She shuddered in the seat and started rocking back and forth, kicking her legs. Her face turned bright red, and then it slowly turned a dark blue. Andrea was a Puerto Rican, and Black mixed chick. So, her skin was fairly light, but I didn't care at this point. I put my hand over her heart and felt it pounding in her chest. She attempted to swallow but could not, this really got her to bouncing around. I held her nose tighter, she passed gas and laid back, shaking. A vein busted in her right eye. Her eyes rolled to the back of her head, as she gave one last kick and went limp. I held her for two minutes and stepped back. I looked down at her feeling sick to my stomach.

Macho came over and placed his hand on my shoulder. "Bruh, don't worry about the body. We'll take care of that. You feel any better?" He looked me over with a concerned face.

I shrugged my shoulders and shook my head. "I don't know man. I feel like I fucked up, that's all."

He stepped in front of me and gave me a hug. "It's life, big homie. Being part of this game, we're destined to lose people. Even ourselves in a matter of time. All we can do is get smarter and try to master the game while we're playing it. Live by the sword, nah' mean?"

Porky yanked, Aaliyah's dead body from the seat and tossed her over his shoulder. "This bitch was trifling. It's gon' feel good to cut her ass up," he scoffed.

* * *

That night, Paper hit me up, and we wound up meeting at, Subway, on thirteenth and Wells street. I had a car full of my hittas roll close behind me. I didn't know what this nigga was on, and I just wanted to be prepared for anything. It turned out that he'd wound up murdering the skinny nigga's brother that I'd hit up a few months back over some missing heroin. The skinny nigga had nigga had gone M.I.A. and was vowing revenge on Paper and myself. At least that was the word I'd heard from Chasity.

I hadn't fucked with, Paper ever since that night, he'd killed Heaven. I didn't see any need to, he was doing his thing and I was flourishing doing mine. I was enjoying the feeling of being alone, being my own man, and making decisions I felt were the right ones. Plus, I liked to lay with women and I didn't some nigga telling me I was being too lovey-dovey or tricking. I hated hearing that shit. I was who I was. I loved to spoil, spend quality time with, and fuck my women.

When I got into the restaurant, Paper was already seated. I noticed four of his hittas sitting in a booth not far from the table he was sitting at. I had two .40 Glocks on my hips. I sized them up real fast and made notes of how I would hit they ass up after I domed, Paper if need be. I slid into the booth, as my hittas walked into Subway, and sat on the other side of the booth where they could see me.

I nodded at them. "What's good, bruh? Long time no see."

Paper was so skinny by this point, I could see the bones in his face. His eyes were bloodshot and dreary. He smelled of musk and that scent that comes from between your thigh and ball area after you've been walking around all day. His hair was nappy, and there were specks of lint all in it. He twitched and smiled at me. I could already smell his breath before he said a word.

"I'm surprised you showed up mister big shot. Thought you was too good to come and fuck wit' a nigga." He scratched his inner forearm. I could see track marks up and down it. It was sad, to say the least. "Shirley dead, she overdosed. Happened yesterday, she still in the attic. I ain't moved her yet." He sucked his teeth and sighed.

"I'm sorry to hear that, bruh. Why you bring me out here?" Seeing him in that state was killing me. I was seconds away from my eyes misting up. I still had love for the homie. I couldn't believe how far he'd fallen, I was glad, I didn't allow him to lead us nowhere.

"It's Bradley and Shaw. They snatched me up and took me down to the station. Got to asking me all kind of questions and shit. Stuff that happened in our crew. It fucked me up how they knew." His breath smelled so bad I was holding mine.

"Shit like what, Paper?" I felt my stomach turn, I was gonna be sick. On the verge of puking. I exhaled and inhaled through my mouth.

"They asked me about Fax, his son, Maxwell, and them other niggas that got stanked a few months back." He picked up the cup that was in front of him and sipped out of it.

I exhaled loudly and looked him over. "Well, what did you say?"

He shrugged his shoulders. "I ain't say shit. I told them that I didn't know what they were talking 'bout. You know I would never get down on you like that. All of them fools had to be dealt with. I supported your decision handling them the way they were handled. It is what it is."

I nodded. "Yeah." I rubbed my chin and looked over my shoulders at his hittas. They looked just as grimy as he did. Their dreads were nappy at the roots. Their eyes were red and glossy. They looked like they stunk. "Bruh, I find that awfully strange that all of the sudden Bradley and Shaw wanna fuck wit' us. They coming at you about murders. If shit was that serious, why they ain't been snatched us up?"

He shrugged his shoulders. "You were running the show, Rich. You said them niggas had to be done in so that's what happened. I know how you get down. Your temper is horrible, had shit not went down the way you said, ain't no telling what you would have done." He sucked his teeth and stood up. "Look, I'm just giving you a heads up on what's good. Hold ya head and be careful. Them people lurking. I'm sure they'll be hollering at you soon."

I watched him leave out of the door. I sat there for a minute trying to clear my mind. I got the feeling that three months was going to be too long of a time to stay in that city. I had to get Aaliyah out of there sooner. She was pregnant with my kid. I owed her my life, from there on out.

Chapter 9

Three weeks later, we opened another club a few blocks from downtown. Chasity had been recruiting a lot of white and Spanish girls to come over to our team. I decided to put most of them in the Garden of Eden downtown, and that was a great idea. Them white folks ate they asses up. They traveled from all around the world and abroad to pay homage to our girls. In less than a month we were seeing no less than thirty thousand every single night except, Sunday. That was a slow day, so I started allowing the strippers to take that day off.

I used that day to have the club thoroughly cleaned. We restocked our alcohol and often held meetings with a few of our outside partners that had made the transition aside for us. Any idea Chasity had I tried my best to Implement them. In the back of my mind, I was thinking that it wouldn't be long before she was running it by herself anyway. I wanted to get out of that city as soon as I could. I started laundering a hundred thousand dollars a week and sending it straight to my Swiss account. I'd opened one in the Caymans for Aaliyah.

One week I'd send a hundred thousand to mine, and the next a hundred thousand to hers. I tried my best to get as close to that quota every single week. My father plugged me with eight kilos of pure China White Heroin. He told me it was mine, and I didn't owe him one red cent. He said he wanted me to master my mafia and get on the way I was supposed to. He'd had the product stuffed into eight mattresses that were delivered to the furniture store in my hood. I was in cahoots with the owner, but not so much so much that he knew what I was getting. His job was to take the five thousand, and call me when beds arrived, which he did with no problem.

I took the eighty kilos, and turned them into a hundred and ten, by mixing them with Fentanyl, and a lot of lactose. When it was all said and done my crops were pure and potent. I flooded the hood right away and kept each one of my traps open twenty-four-hours a day. I didn't shut down shop until whichever trap my workers were rocking out of went completely dry. A few hours later, a delivery was made, and that same trap was back jumping like LeBron.

Around this same time, the Misfits had completely taken over, Hillside Row houses. They'd kicked in doors, and reigned down terror on the residents that stayed there. After they'd completely rid it of the Spanish Flies they cornered the drug market on every angle. They placed an order to me for a hundred kilos of heroin at a price of ten gees a piece, and fifty of The Andrea. That was my mix of Meth and Cocaine that Andrea taught me how to whip up. I let it be known, that they didn't owe me a penny up front. I would pick up my money every Friday, as they made it. Before long the Misfits was going hard and making money hand over fist.

My father had me sit down with a cartel Boss by the name of, Cabo. He was a well-known, dark, and jitty drug lord from the heart of Mexico City. Everything coming into the United States via Mexico, Florida, or Canada, he had his hand in the middle of it. He was a short man with a bushy mustache and small eyes. His skin was brownish red, and he spoke with a strong accent. For the meeting, my pops flew us out in his private jet to Brazil. I sat back in the soft leather seat, the chair vibrated, and massaged my shoulders.

I'd had a nice piece of triple cheese Lasagna and garlic bread. Then washed it down with a bottle of Ace of Spades. I followed that up with a blunt of Veracruz Weed from the heart of Mexico. Two, beautiful, Mexican women made sure me and my father were, well taken care of, as we sat on the plane flying over the states below.

My father took a sip from his glass, then he pursed his lips, and set it back down. "Son, this will be your first official meeting with a true Boss. Now that you are moving as much dope as you are. You must get the permission from Dons across the map. You have my blessing, but even I have to answer to men in this underworld. Everyone has somebody to answer to. It's a completely different ball game. One that you must respect the rules of, or it can cost you your life, and the lives of the ones you truly love."

One of the Mexican stewardesses brought him a Cuban cigar, with the end already clipped off. He took it, and she lit the tip for him, smoke wafted into the air. She smiled and walked away with her ass switching from right to left.

"Your name is ringing in the underworld, Rich. Cabo wants to know what kind of man you are. He hears good things, but it's not enough. You must approach him with the utmost respect and think before you speak. Any sign of weakness will reflect not only you but myself as well. You have my stamp of approval and that holds a lot of weight. Lastly, do not let him find out, you're my son. He'll cry a case of nepotism, we don't need that. I need you to be your own man in this game."

I watched the clouds float by outside the window. It was bright and sunny over the area we were flying. I was thinking about, Aaliyah more than what he was saying to me. We had a doctor's appointment scheduled two days from this day. I just wanted to be by her side for it. That was my job.

I took a sip of the champagne. "Pop, I got this, I understand you're a lil' worried, but it's good. I know how to hold my own, always have. I'ma treat this dude just like I'd expect to be treated. It's as simple as that." I took a pull off the blunt and inhaled. I was missing Aaliyah.

My father sat back in his seat and shrugged his shoulders. Three big muscled bound guards were stationed around the plane with scowls on their faces. My father pulled one of the stewardesses down onto his lap.

She giggled and wiggled her bottom on him. "Que Paso, Senor Paulie."

He squeezed her thigh and slid his hand under her skirt. His arm began to move back and forth, as she started moaning out loud in heavy gasps.

"Son, you are a man now. I have full faith in you to do what is expected. I've never held your hand, and I won't start, right now." He nodded and snapped his fingers. "Enjoy yourself."

The second stewardess came over and tried to sit on my lap, but I stopped her. "I'm good, shawty. I ain't on that, right now."

She looked down at me confused, then placed her hand on her hip, and shrugged her shoulders, before sitting on my father's lap, unbuttoning her blouse.

I pulled out my phone and called, Aaliyah. I just wanted to make sure she was straight. I needed to hear her voice to calm my soul. I spent the rest of the flight to Brazil on the phone with her. Her voice was like food to my soul.

* * *

The meeting was held in a swampy dungeon. In order to get inside of it, we had to travel up a big hill, riding Mopeds. We rolled past a bunch of the locals that looked poor and starving. Their homes consisted of brittle shacks, with aluminum roofs. The streets were narrow on each side of us. There seemed to be a whole community of people outside. Even though, the sun was beaming worse than ever. It was super humid. We had to dodge more than five different soccer balls that rolled into the street. Kids chased us for sometime laughing and begging for money. While others had weapons in their hands looking for an opportunity to rob us. They were frail and looked malnourished.

When we made it to the middle of the big hill. I noticed there were clouds all around us. I began to panic deep within my mind. I knew I couldn't let my father see it, but he looked just as sick. We hopped off the mopeds when we came to a cave. Once there we were ordered to switch over to four-wheelers. Six armed guards were in front of the cave with AK47's against their shoulders.

They searched us thoroughly before we could get on the four-wheelers and drive into the cave. It got cool as soon as we were about ten yards inside of it. It was dark, and I could hear bats flapping overhead. I felt itchy, and a little on edge. I didn't know nothing about Brazil. My father's men had been made to stay outside, and we'd been searched so good that it was impossible for us to bring anything along with us. I felt at the mercy of the Brazilians. I didn't like it one bit. The big lights on top of the four-wheeler illuminated our path. More than a few times bats flew close enough to my face, I could smell the stink of them. I swung at them, missing by inches. I couldn't wait until we got to our destination.

Ten minutes later, and after exiting the four-wheelers and getting searched from head to toe once again. We were led into a big arena, where Cabo sat in the middle of, with twenty armed guards behind him. In front of the table were seven men hanging from big metal hooks by their wrists that were roped around. Cabo stood when he saw us.

My father walked in his direction with his hand extended. They met and shook. I was two paces behind my father. "Cabo, it's good to see you again, man. It's been a while."

He shook and smiled, looking over my father's shoulders. "And this must be the rich kid from the hood. I've heard a lot about you, kid. I take it Don Paulie has brought you up to speed with who I am?" he stepped past my father and shook my hand.

I shook his. "Yes, he has. It's an honor to meet you, Senor Cabo."

He smiled, and opened his hand, asking us to sit without saying the words. We took our seats at the long table. He walked around to the other side and sat across from us. There was a man on each side of him. They eyed us with hatred and didn't say a word. Cabo took his seat and waved his hand in the air. Out of the shadows came five women with tight black shirts and white blouses that were so snug I could make out the areolas on their breasts. They covered the table with all kinds of food. Along with fresh fruit, and Champagne, they set one dish in front of Cabo, in a metal tray with a covering. He nodded at them, and they disappeared back into the shadows.

It felt like soggy dirt under my feet, I could see all kinds of insects crawling beneath us. It smelled like wet earth all around, and there were still seven men hanging from ropes behind us. It freaked me out a little bit, but I kind of liked Cabo's swagger. He gave off deadly vibes, cold, and raw. I dug the whole set up and couldn't wait to see what this meeting was all about.

He smiled, "Rich, you've been moving a lot of kilo throughout Milwaukee. I would say, that you've made quite a pretty penny for yourself. Have you not?" He grabbed a glass and poured some red wine into it. Then he slid it across the table to me.

The men on each side of him looked at me as if they wished I died before them. I could tell they were waiting for me to say the wrong thing, so they could snuff me.

I nodded my head. "It's been quite a ride on my way to the top. I'm eating, but it could be better."

Cabo laughed. "You hear this, Vato?" He asked the man to the right of him never taking his eyes off me. "He sounds like a greedy son of a bitch, doesn't he?" Cabo lowered his eyes and looked from my father to me. "You've moved hundreds of kilos. Killed off a bunch of the Spanish Flies, then flooded their territory with your dope. Now you have not only their people hooked on it but yours as well. I'd say you're doing quite alright for yourself."

I grabbed one of the grapes and tossed it into my mouth. It tasted a little sweet and sour. I chewed it and nodded my head. "Something tells me that all of this questioning's leading somewhere?" I grabbed another grape and ate it.

Cabo stood up and held out his right hand. One of his armed guards came over and placed a machete in it. He scooted his chair back, walked over to one of the seven hanging men, took the tape from his mouth and dropped into the dirt. The man started screaming something in a foreign language. He began shaking and twisting against his binds. He was butt naked, with blood dripping from his mouth. He looked as if he were 'bout forty years old. A businessman of some sort.

Cabo mugged me. "There's only one problem with you doing what you were doing, Rich. I didn't give you permission to soar as high as you have. Somebody has to answer for that mistake. Just like this peasant right here. He had the nerve to make a hundred million dollars off cocaine, that my Cartel supplied and didn't send me one penny. How do you think that makes me feel?" He faced the man, raised the machete over his head and slammed into the man's torso with two hands, and drug it inward, splitting him in two. I watched his insides fall, it was so gut-wrenching that I had to rub my head. Now I was getting a lil' worried. I felt like me and my old man was under the gun. I began to fidget in my chair, I felt a big ant crawling up my leg and shook it off. Then I started feeling itchy all over and sweat decorated my forehead. I had never been more nervous in my life.

Cabo walked over with blood dripping from the blade of the machete. He wiped it on my father's shirt, looking him in the eyes. "You have vouched for this black kid. That means that his sins are your hands. Your soul in the underworld. How do you look to rectify this, old friend?" He placed his hands on my shoulders.

My father smiled and grabbed his glass of wine. "He's a good kid. I take full responsibility for his transgressions. As a show of apology, I am looking to compromise." He swallowed the entire glass of wine, then poured him another.

I was beginning to think that my pops was an alcoholic or something. I wasn't feeling how he drank, I saw it as a sign of weakness.

Cabo stepped in front of the second man, raised the machete, and sliced him down the middle, just as he'd done the first victim. The man's blood skeeted out of him and splattered into Cabo's face.

Cabo walked over and wiped it on my cheek. "And what compromise can you make for me Don Paulie, I'm all ears? As you can see I've cleared two spots on my hooks for fresh meat. I think you and this Mayate could fit quite well up there."

My father frowned and adjusted himself in his seat. He looked fire hot, I think he must've known what Cabo called me in Spanish, but at the time I didn't. I was more heated about this punk putting blood on my cheek. Aaliyah was pregnant, and I didn't want to expose her to anything. I'd already broken a condom while fucking, Poverty. Even though they were swearing that I was her first I wasn't so sure.

"It just came down from the courts that gambling is legal is in all fifty states. Are you, familiar with this?" My father asked him, running his fingers through his silky black hair.

Cabo shrugged his shoulders. "Yeah, I heard about that, but what does that have to do with me? I am a drug lord."

My father smiled a crooked grin. I could tell he didn't like, Cabo at this time. I could see his face turning red and everything. I was wondering how it must've been for him to sit back and listen to Cabo be so disrespectful. My father was a plugged man in his own right.

"Now that I am in the wings of becoming the official Don of the Bertolli family. I have access to two very important one-hundred million dollars a year grossing strips. One in Las Vegas, and one in Atlantic City. That's two-hundred million a year. I'm willing to cut you in on twenty-five percent of the real estate. That's a cool fifty million a year, depending on how you use the space. It could be more. You will have full backing and I'll make sure you are led in the right direction. That's my word to you, Cabo."

Cabo leaned over my chair and placed his sweaty palm on top of my waves. "You'll do all of that for this black hijo de puta?" He smiled and nodded his head. "Well, it'd be stupid of me to pass up such an opportunity. Long as you follow through on your word and this Bastard can kick in what he owes to me monthly, we shouldn't have any more problems. In fact, I have an idea. I'm going to do something that might just make all three of us a lot of money." He picked up the bottle of Champagne from the table and sipped out of it.

Behind me, I could hear the guts of the hanging men that he'd sliced open falling on to the ground. The men sounded as if they were gurgling on their blood. It was enough to drive a man crazy. I was ready to get out of there, and as far away from Brazil as possible.

My father nodded and looked up to, Cabo. "Let's hear it."

"Since this Black kid has made such an impact in a small city like Milwaukee in such little time. How about we use his skin complexion, and intelligence to venture out into the cities to do business with Blacks. He understands their street lingos like I understand Spanish." He laughed and popped a grape into his mouth, he chewed it and looked from my father, then to me. "Keep in mind that everything he does he'll have to answer to me at the end of the month. I'll fulfill any order he can handle at sixty percent, he pays nothing up front. He books the order the order, and I'll supply it. One way or another, you're talking millions from the gambling. I'm talking millions from my field of expertise. You understand me?"

My father nodded at him. He turned to me and place his hand on my knee. "Are you ready to step into an arena as big as the one he's offering you? This could spell millions in a short amount of time."

I wiped some of the blood off my cheek and sucked my teeth looking up at Cabo. I thought about what the money would mean for Kesha, Aaliyah, our child and even myself. I'd always wanted to be my own boss and buss major moves on my own account. Now I was being offered the game in a way that most didn't. I knew I was ready. I didn't care what came along with it. I would adjust. I'd do whatever it took to provide for my family and those that I cared about. It was my obligation as a man.

I looked into my father's eyes and nodded. "Hell, yeah, I'm ready, Pop. Let me do this."

He searched my eyes for a long time without saying a word. "Cabo, he has my support. I feel he is ready to step into the big leagues." He sat back in his chair, after picking a strawberry off the platter of fruit, and eating it, then smiled at me.

Cabo tapped me on the shoulder. "Stand up."

I made my way to my feet and wiped the rest of the blood off my cheek. I felt angered and disgusted at the same time. He placed his arm around my shoulders and walked me down the line of the seven hanging men. When he got in front of the black dude, with long dreads.

He stopped and looked up at him. "This the last Black man that I put my faith and product into. New York, Chicago, Los Angeles, Dallas and every city that is dominated by your people in between. I placed all those drug markets at his feet. Told him to get rich and just pay my sixty percent monthly. No harm no foul." He laughed while still looking up at him. "But this stupid muthafucka tried to double cross me and run to Haiti." He scrunched his face and handed me the Machete that was in his right hand. "If you want the power that he had, you take this, and you kill him, just as I've killed those down there." He pointed toward the carnage he'd created.

The men's intestines hung out of them and dripped blood into the soil. I took the Machete, looked over the hanging man, and felt nothing. It was what it was. He was standing in a position that I needed more than he did.

"Go." Cabo took a step back and smiled.

I raised the machete over my head like he had with two hands and brought it down with all my might into the man's chest and sliced downward. Ripping through his midsection, all the way through his balls. His insides poured out of him and down to the soil in a heap of steam and blood.

Cabo clapped his hands together and placed his arm back around my neck. "Never let him become you. Here's how things are gonna go."

Chapter 10

It wasn't more than two weeks after I'd officially plugged in with, Cabo, and I was slanging kilos of pure heroin and cocaine, not only in Milwaukee, but I moved a hundred a week down to Chicago, a hundred to St. Louis, a hundred to Detroit, a hundred to Cleveland, Atlanta, and even Dallas. The process kick-started faster than I felt I was ready for. I felt like I was losing my mind until my father stepped away from his Mafia and came alongside me to teach me a system that would burst work for me and the demands I had all over the United States. It was because of him that I never delivered more than a hundred kilos a week to any city.

He said it wouldn't be smart to put too much of my footprint in one spot. I had to leave room for other drug lords to move some of their product. To corner the markets totally would bring on too much hatred and spell disaster. The last thing I needed was to go to war with any major dealers while I was still getting established. Cabo didn't care what I got into, or how much I got into it, with anybody. He expected to have four million dollars a month wired into his account in the Caymans no later than the thirtieth of each month. No excuses. He didn't care if I was in prison, or in a hospital. If I was still alive I was responsible for his product, and the payment of it.

I started recruiting dope boys in every major city I served to. I snatched, up them grimy niggas that were starving. They were my caliber. I made sure I put a government like system in place so that rules were implemented and followed. If anyone of my rules was broken, I was having your ass gunned down or beheaded. I figured since my life was on the line from fucking with Cabo.

Then every nigga I put on life was too. It was how the game went, and I had very little problems because I set examples in each city straight out the gate. I massacre a mufucka publicly in front of my dope boys and his family. Niggas wasn't trying to see that fate, so they stayed in line and ate as much as they could.

I made sure to keep all their home addresses and the addresses of the main people in their lives. I made sure I had niggas being monitored and that the ones monitoring them, were also being monitored. After, Cabo's four million a month, I was seeing about two for myself. That's not counting the money coming from the strip clubs and the dope my pops had given me before I linked up with Cabo. If all of that was added, I was seeing about three point five million a month.

I strengthened the businesses in my ghetto by upgrading their material and fixing up the outside and the inside as well. I snatched up more than a hundred sistas out of the hood and put them in salons, restaurants, clothing stores, cell phone shops, and even massage parlors. I made sure they were paid a decent wage, and in addition to their paychecks, I took care of their rent, and car notes, as long as they purchased their vehicles from one of the three car dealerships that my pops had helped me purchase. I just wanted to see my people thrive and get in a better position. I knew it started with the women in my old community.

For the men, I bought five used school buses, painted them, threw a system inside each one and added televisions in the back of each headrest. The buses were used to take the women to go and see their men in prison four times a week, as long as they signed up for it forty-eight hours in advance. I set it up so that my crew paid phone bills for the homies to call home as much as they could. We hired ten really good defense attorneys. So, that when the homies got into a jam all they had to do was hit up one of my generals and they would be there to help them any way they could.

Our businesses in our hood was to hire the people from our hood. Everybody had to work, if I found out they were reaping the benefits without contributing to the cause, they were put on sanctions until they got their minds right. No mother was able to come to me and say her house was not filled with food, nice clothes, and everything that she needed. I wasn't having that at all. My first priority was the women and children.

In three months, my community looked completely different. Everybody was driving nice cars and had grass in front of their homes. The streets was no longer filled with litter and paraphernalia from drug usage. It seemed as if our people were starting to love where they came from. I knew that it was my job to keep on pouring into them all.

In the fourth month, I came home one Thursday night, to find Aaliyah sitting in the middle of the living room, with candles burning all around her. Her eyes were closed, she sat crossed legged Indian style. I had a duffle bag over my shoulder with five hundred thousand dollars in cash, and ten bricks of Cabo's tar heroin. I'd been gone for three days straight, traveling with my hustlers, delivering weight to different cities. I was tired and worn out, I just wanted to lay beside her and get some sleep. She rubbed her naked belly that looked like a pretty brown watermelon while breathing in and out of her nose.

I squatted down and kissed her on the cheek. She leaned her head to the side to receive it. "How you doing, Lil' mama?"

She shook her head, and slowly opened her eyes. "It's time for us to go, Rich. This is the fourth month now."

I kissed her stomach and rubbed it for a second. "That's your response?" I scoffed, and stood back up, grabbed my bag and walked into our Master bedroom.

I turned the bag upside down and dumped the five hundred thousand in cash along with the ten kilos of heroin. I shoved the dresser out of the way and slid the wall to the side. Then I punched in the code on my safe and waited for it to pop open. Aaliyah walked into the room with her pretty toes and big belly. She ran her fingers through her curly hair, she'd done. She looked real good to me. Her navel was poking out and her stomach was dark brown. I loved this girl so fucking much. The fact that she was having my seed only added to my appreciation of her.

"Did you just ignore what I said and walk away from me?" She asked looking me up and down irritated.

I started loading my safe, grabbing the stacks forcing them into it. This was one of nine safes I had, each safe couldn't hold more than a million in them. The five hundred thousand would push it to its limit. So that meant I had to put the kilos in a different safe. I sighed because I really didn't want to argue with my woman. I didn't like stressing her out while she was pregnant. Lately, it seemed like she needed to vent more.

"Baby, I ain't ignore you, I just gotta get this bread up. Then we can sit down and get right to it." I think that was the thing I really loved about, Aaliyah the fact that the money and dope didn't impress her. She would have loved me even if I was broke, I truly believed that.

She kneeled with her big stomach and began helping me load the safe. "Baby, I think it's time that we move on. You said we'd be out of here in three months. I kept my mouth shut and gave you and gave you an extra month. I knew you had to get the money right before we left. But look at this, we have money everywhere. In safes, in foreign accounts, tucked away in mattresses and in your sister's name. We don't need any more fucking money. It's time to go I want to have this child in a different place. A place where there isn't too much bad history." She looked inside the safe that was as tall as half a refrigerator. Her tummy looked freshly oiled.

I shook my head. "Maybe you're right, bae. I ain't really gotta confine myself to this city anymore. Our money is spread out. I did promise you we'd be out in three months. I dislike lying to you, even though I had to make this all happen." I sighed and stuffed the last stack inside the safe and waited for her to do the same with her bundle. I closed it back after she finished. Wheeled it into the wall, and slid the wall back in front of it, followed by the dresser. I helped her to her feet and rubbed her pretty face. "You're really ready to go huh, baby?"

She nodded. "I'm not happy here. I've been ready to go since the first time you told me, you loved me. I just want you all to myself. I want us to raise our child together and live happily ever after. You're the king baby, nobody can dispute that. Let's get out of here."

I smiled, kissed her on the forehead, wrapped her into my arms, and held her for a minute. She smelled of Gild Bonds Coco butter oil. I knew she was trying her best to prevent getting too many stretch marks, but I didn't care if she got them or not. I was gon' love her for the rest of my life.

"Baby, everything I do now, is so I can give you and Kesha a better life. Nothing makes me happier than knowing that you two will never need for anything for as long as you're alive. I appreciate you for nourishing my seed. I know it takes a lot out of you every single day. I know it ain't easy being involved wit' a man like me, but, I thank God for you. You are the truth on every single level." I rubbed her cheeks with my thumbs. "If you're really ready to go, so am I. Question is, where are you thinking?"

She looked into my eyes and bit her bottom lip. "Daddy, honestly, I'll go anywhere with you. As long as I know, that you are my man, and you'll be home at night to sleep beside me. We could move into a cardboard box, because for me it's not about what we have, it's about the love you have for me. I've been through so much. You have been my healing hand, my oasis. I feel like I need you just to breathe these days, but to answer your question let's move to Houston. I've been researching their real estate market down there and I feel like I could make a lot of lead way. Texas, period, it can be a new start for us, in a new state. You can open a few businesses down there, and we can live in a gated community. What do you say?"

I held her, rubbing all over that big pregnant booty. It was poked out a lil' further too and putting a hurting on the material of her Gucci skirt. I leaned down, and kissed her exposed stomach, rubbing my face along the skin. "I say we on our way to Texas, baby. I'ma let you pick the area, the house whatever you want. It's all about what will make you happy. That's all I care about."

She wrapped her arms around the top of my neck and stomped her right foot two times, fighting back tears as her eyes misted over. She swallowed and winced. "Baby, I love you so much! I swear I thank God for you every single day. You are an amazing man. I don't understand why you've chosen me to be your woman, but I also know that I'm not supposed to question his blessings. I just want to be the absolute best woman, I can be to you. The best mother I can be to our child and lend my prayers up to our Father in Heaven." Tears leaked out of her pretty brown eyes. They ran down on my fingers and I wipe them away.

I nodded. "I love you too, Boo. I thank Him for you just as much. You're my Queen. All I see is you and will from here on out." I laughed and cuffed that ass real good. "Been a while since I tasted my baby, though. Sit yo' lil' self or this bed and let me eat that pregnant thang for a minute. Remind me why you got me so hooked on this body."

She held her stomach, and slowly backed over to the bed. Then she sat down, and pulled her skirt up, exposing her thick thighs. She was without panties. Since she'd been pregnant she allowed the hairs to grow on her pussy. I'd shave it for her every two weeks or so. if I didn't shave it, it didn't get done. She was spoiled like that, by this point. But true love a get a nigga like she had me. I made her place both of her feet on the bed and opened her thighs as wide as they would go. I turned my head sideways because her belly was in her lap a lil' bit. I sniffed that pretty pussy, then sucked it into my mouth. I pulled both lips apart and slid my tongue into her crease, licking up and down, while I held the lips apart.

"Mmm-daddy, it feels so good. It feels so-so good," she moaned and sucked her bottom lip.

I slurped and licked up and down over and over. I sucked her clit and nipped at it with my teeth, flicked my tongue back and forth across it, then sucked it again. Tasting her juices letting them go down my throat. The scent of Coco Butter wafted up my nose. I stuck my nose into her hole and inhaled. Trapped her sex lips into my mouth and enjoyed pleasing my baby. I appreciated her, and I just wanted her to know it.

"I love you, baby! Mmm," I sucked at her clit.

She arched her back and dug her nails into my shoulders. "I love you too-Daddy. Uhh-baby, I love you so, so much, uhh oooh-wee." She pulled up her top to reveal her plump breasts. The nipples were engorged, and shiny on their tips. She pulled on them and squeezed her breasts together while riding my face slowly.

She leaned onto her side and I really got to attacking that cat. I sucked and licked in between her sex lips like a maniac. I needed to taste her better. I wanted her to cum all over my tongue and lips. I needed her too. I was feening for it like never before. I nipped at her clit and sucked it so hard into my mouth that she lifted her left thigh, held it in the air, and pulled my face into her box, while she laid on her side.

"Uh, eat me, daddy. Eat your baby. I'm finna cum. I'm finna cum on you," she whimpered, riding my face faster and faster.

The bed squeaked, the headboard tapped against the wall. She dug her nails into the bed, and tightened her thighs around my head, riding me hard. I could barely breathe, but needed for her to cum, she deserved, too. I wanted to eat it up. I slapped her ass and wormed my finger into her hole back there. That was all it took to send her over the edge. She screamed at the top of her lungs, threw her head back, and came all over my mouth and face, squirting her juices like a squirt gun. I felt it running down my neck and into the collar of my shirt. I licked up as much as I could, swallowing the taste of my pregnant woman, knowing that I'd made her happy.

After I was done, she laid on her side and searched properties and moving locations, in Texas, on her laptop. I rubbed that big ass the whole time and laid my head on her the scent of her pussy until I passed out from exhaustion.

Hood Rich

Chapter 11

The Misfits had not only taken complete control over the Hill Side Row Houses, but in less than three months, they'd conquered Lapham Park which was another community of Row Houses ten blocks away. Lapham Park was considered Heroin Addict Haven. It seemed like four out of ten of the people that lived there were addicts. The Misfits were copping fifty kilos from me every nine days. I charged them twenty a piece for heroin. It got to the point where I was no longer fronting them the work and picking up my money on Fridays, but they were already wiring me the upfront by Zelle. It got to the point that I was wiring them every time we met. I had to applaud their hustle.

One day, as me and Aaliyah, was coming out of Harry Winston's. I'd just bought her a two-carat raspberry diamond engagement ring. We were headed back to my black on black, 2019 Jaguar that I had sitting on twenty-six-inch gold rims. I popped up the Lamborghini door for, Aaliyah to slide into, when Macho rolled up behind me in a black on black Hummer, binging out of control. It sounded like a concert coming out If his whip. We were in a parking garage. He jumped out to approach my driver's side, but before he could he was swarmed by ten of my hittas that were on security. They ran at him with Tech .9s ready to empty their clips like I'd ordered them to do if ever they felt I was in danger.

Macho upped two .40 Calibers with extended clips and lowered his eyes into slits. "Let's get it fuck niggas!"

I stuffed Aaliyah into the car and slammed the door. "That's my lil' homie!" I yelled. Macho's men jumped out of the truck with Uzzi's. Our men were at a standoff. "Y'all chill, I ain't gon' say that shit again," I snapped.

Macho waved his men off. They slowly got back into his hummer and slammed their doors. He placed his guns back into their holsters and walked over to me.

He gave me a hug and we shook up. "What it do, Boss?" he asked smiling.

I shook my head. "Chilling, I gotta drop my Lil' One off. I know you wanna sit down and holler at me, but I gotta make sure she straight first. You wanna meet up later tonight?"

He nodded and looked past me into my Jaguar. "Yeah, that sounds good. How about we meet at Mr. Chow's, that lil' Chinese joint off Michigan Avenue? Say like seven?"

I gave him a hug and patted his back. "That sounds good, bruh. I'll see you then."

When I got back in the car, I noticed that Aaliyah had her hand inside her Birkin bag. She had a 9-millimeter clutched tightly, with tears running down her face.

I frowned. "Baby, what's the matter?" I looked her over closely.

"I'm tired of going through this stuff, Rich. I don't want to live this life anymore. I keep on thinking that today will be our last day. It's driving me nuts." Her hand was shaking.

I felt my heart skip a beat. I felt sick to my stomach. I didn't realize how much me being in the game was really negatively affecting her. I knew I had to get her out of that city. Her sanity depended on it.

"Look, baby, I promise. We're out of here, give me three weeks, and it's a wrap. You got my word on that." I kissed her cheek. "Put your seat belt on."

She swallowed. "Three weeks, Rich, *three* weeks is all I can take."

I started up my whip, waiting for one of the cars filled with my hittas to pull out in front of me. Then I pulled out and the two remaining cars filled with them followed close behind me. I kept on checking on, Aaliyah. I hated seeing her in that state of mind, I wished we could have left earlier.

* * *

Macho opened the package to his chopsticks and looked across the table at me, smiling. "You good over there, Boss?"

I was sitting in front of a barbecued platter, and I didn't even have an appetite. I actually felt sick more than anything else. I had Aaliyah on my mind real heavy.

I nodded my head. "I'm good, lil', bruh. And stop calling me, Boss nigga. You eating just as much as I am now. You're your own boss. We're at eye level, I love it, too." I popped the cork on the bottle of Moet.

He shook his head. "Naw, nigga, I wish. I got cousins down in St. Louis that's flooding their hood with your shit. Porky's folks in Dallas doing the same thing. You got a whole bunch of niggas eating off you, Big Homie. That's why the slums calling you Hood Rich. You're what we aspire to be in this game. I'll never forget how you put me and my crew on real talk. Loyalty is a mutha-fucka, believe that." He tilted his glass, so I could pour champagne into it.

I laughed. "Yeah, a'ight. I love you, too, lil' homie. So, what's good?" I picked up a piece of the barbecue and wanted to see if my stomach would hold it.

"Me and Porky butting heads. The money starting to make us look at each other differently. There some tension in the air and I don't like it. That ain't all, either." He shook his head as he lowered it. "I fucked up, and I don't know if I should tell you what I did. I can't have you judging me and shit." He exhaled loudly and sat back in his chair.

My stomach began to turn as soon as I swallowed the meat. I had to stay away from that for a minute. At least until I was able to console my Lil' One. I was hoping that she was resting at that moment. "Holler at me lil', bruh. It ain't nothing you gon' tell me that would make me turn my back on you. You and Porky are like my lil' brothers. I'd bleed for you lil' niggas with no hesitation. We've all been through a lot together. You should know that I'ma hold you down, unconditionally."

Macho lowered his head again and exhaled loudly. He covered his face with one hand and sat back. Mr. Chow's restaurant was crowded with mostly white people. You were given the option to sit on the floor, or at a table. Most of the people there were seated on nice clean carpets with a short but long table in front of them to accommodate their meals and drinks. The waiters hurried from place to the next to keep the customers happy. The lights were dimmed and in the background was the sound of Chinese music. To me, it was relaxing and soothing. I felt like I was in a karate movie.

"Spit it out, lil, bruh. I ain't gon' say it again."

Once again Macho sighed loudly. "I got Porky's sister pregnant. She ain't showing yet, but when she start, that nigga gonna wanna chop something down. He tooting that blow real heavy now, mix all that shit with them pills, and his drinking. His judgment ain't been the best on many levels. I can't leave out the part about her being sixteen either." Just then started avoiding my eye contact.

I put my elbow on the table and held my forehead. I didn't know what to say. Had I found out that, Paper was fucking with anyone of my sisters before they turned eighteen and got them pregnant. Man, I think I would have killed him. I imagine that. Though I would have preferred, Keyonna to have been pregnant then dead.

"Well, ain't you gon' say something?" He asked staring at me.

I shrugged my shoulders. "Nigga, you bogus. You know you are. That's his little sister. I'm pretty sure he's been doing everything he can to keep her away from danger, right?"

Macho, nodded. "Yeah. He don't allow nobody around her, but me. He says he wants her to do something with her life. Both of us are trying to follow your playbook. You sent your sister off to college and what not? That's admirable." He shook his head. "What should I do? Do I tell him or what?"

I drank out of the Champagne and sat back. "Bruh, you've grown up with him ever since y'all was what age?"

"Five."

"That's thirteen years. You should know him better than anybody?"

"Yeah, well you and Paper got the same relationship. If something like that happened between you and him, would you tell him what was good? Or would you keep it to yourself, and figure things out on the low?"

"Do you love his sister, be honest?"

Macho shrugged his shoulders. "I don't know, I kinda love my lady that I got at home with my daughter.

She's been with me since day one. Even chopped up a few hoodies with me. She's my rider, Mariella is just so beautiful, she reminds me of Shakira. I've never in my life seen someone so fine. Her body is amazing as well and she's so smart for her age. I guess being around her so much, things just started to shape, and one thing led to another. I don't want to lose, Porky over is." He swallowed and blinked his eyes repeatedly.

I could tell the situation was getting to him more than he was letting on. He couldn't stay still his eyes scanned the entire restaurant.

"I say you tell him what's good. Just keep it real with him. And you gone have to give him more than what you just gave me. You expect him to accept that you were thinking she was so fine, you couldn't stay away from her. That makes you sound like a predator. It's not a good look."

Macho nodded his head. "Yeah, you're right. Well, I'ma do that, but I want you to do me a favor. Can you be there when I tell him? He looks up to you. I think he'll hear you out more than he would me at this point."

* * *

That Saturday night, I invited the Misfits bosses and Porky, to The Garden of Eden, and made sure that they were supreme V.I.P. treatment. I had them ducked off in a private room on the second level, right above the main stage. Two dancers Poverty and Magic sat on their laps and gave them slow lap dances, while I sat across from them drinking a bottle of Dom Perignon and smoking a big blunt.

I was high, and a little drunk, *Drake's 'Nice for What'* banged out of the speakers, while Poverty and Magic did their thing. Chasity stepped into the private room and sat on my lap. She wore a skin-tight Balienci suit that clung to her every curve. She sat on my lap, wrapped her arm around my neck, and leaned in for a kiss, but I moved my head out of reach.

She frowned and jerked her head backward. "What's the matter with you?" She sounded angry.

I shook my head. "Nothing, I'm trying to do right by, Aaliyah, that's all. She about to pop out my kid, and I just put that ring on her finger. Time to be on some grown man shit now. She deserves that."

Chasity sucked her teeth. "Boy!" She kissed my lips and licked them. "I ain't trying to break up yo' happy home. Congratulations! Long as you give me some of this dick when I need it. I couldn't care less who you marry. Straight up." She kissed my cheek and rose from my lap. Her big ass was all in my face.

I couldn't do nothing but shake my head. I already saw that temptations were going to be the hardest part to conquer. Especially being around so many bad, aggressive ass women. Not one of the females in either one of my clubs were less than a dime. I made sure of that.

"Yo', Poverty, Magic, y'all leave us alone for a while. I gotta holler at my niggas."

Poverty stood up and Macho's hands fell from her ass that was encased in a pink thong. The cheeks were decorated with freckles. She walked away with both cheeks jiggling like crazy. She looked over her shoulder and blinked at me.

Magic was caramel-skinned and super bad. She was from Memphis and strapped like all she ate was soul food and did crunches all day long. Her body was strapped, yet she ain't have no stomach. The first day she walked into the club I wanted to kill that shit, but I hadn't. Aaliyah was getting to me. She stood up, and Porky pulled his fingers out of her pussy. He stuck them into his mouth and slapped her ass. She yelped and walked bowlegged out of the room. Both had left with ten thousand knots and I would hit them with two gees later for entertaining my homies.

I got up and closed the door behind her. Then I lowered the blinds in the room and took my seat. "A'ight, bruh, I just wanna let y'all know that I love both of you. I'd do anything for either one of you in a heartbeat. That being said, I feel like we're all family. And sometimes in a family, there are things that are hard to get over and past, but it's something that must be done." I looked from Porky to Macho.

Porky laughed, picked up a bottle of Patron from the table and turned it up. His Adam's apple moved up and down. When he set the once full bottle back down, it was now half gone. He burped and wiped his mouth with the back of his hand. "Say what's on your mind, Hood Rich, damn."

I nodded at Macho. "Hear lil' homie out."

Macho stood up and sighed. He grabbed the bottle of Patron from the table and turned it up. "A'ight, Porky, I did something that I know ain't gon' sit right wit' you, bruh. I want to apologize ahead of time. I swear I'm gon' make things right. All you gotta do is give me a chance."

Porky scrunched his face and looked up to me. He mugged Macho and ran his chubby hand over his face. "What the fuck you, niggas keeping from me, huh? You got something you need to say to me, Macho. You say it.

You're getting me hot, Ese." He rubbed the palms of his hands on his jeans.

Macho sat on the couch across from him. He exhaled slowly and shook his head. "It's Mariella."

Porky scrunched his face harder and mugged, Macho. "What about, Mariella, Homes?"

"Bruh, I know you trusted me. She's like my sister and we've grown up together. But I fucked up. I just hope you can forgive me and give me a chance to do what I need too. Because I—"

Porky lowered his eyes. "What the fuck are you saying, Ese? All I hear are a bunch of words that aren't making any sense. What the fuck does, Mariella, have to do with anything?" He hollered as his double chin shook.

"I got her pregnant, Porky! I screwed up and got her pregnant. I didn't mean to it just happened, bruh. I'm sorry, but you know, I'm going to handle my responsibility for her. She's like my kid sister just as much as yours."

Porky sat on the couch clenching his jaw. It was like I could see steam coming from the top of his head. He nodded and looked up at me. "How long did you know about this?"

"Just a few days, bruh. He came to me with it, and I thought I should be present when he told you. I'm just here as the big brother. That's it." I sat back on the couch and looked him over. I was so high, I could barely keep my eyes open.

Porky turned to Macho and smiled. "We're brothers' man. I've never had a friend other than you. You're the only person I trust in this life and in the next. Even more than Santa Maria." He was quiet for a long time. *The Migos, 'Stir Fry'*, boomed out of the speakers. The room felt eerie and odd. I didn't know what to say to break the tension.

"I'm sorry man. I swear to God, I'm sorry," Macho pleaded.

Porky pulled his nose. "She's my little sister, only have one. She wants to go off to college, so she can become a doctor. The first one in the family. I've put two hundred thousand away for her, now this," he scoffed. "My right-hand man at that." He shook his head. "Well, I can't really blame you, Hood Rich. Thank you for encouraging him to tell me." He leaned over and shook my hand, and then it was like everything happened in slow motion. His face turned into a scowl. He jumped up, pulled out two .45s, cocked them, and let 'em rip into

Macho's face, and torso.

Boom! Boom! Boom! Boom! Boom! Boom!

The guns jumped in his hands again and again as fire spit out of the barrels. Smoke wafted into the air and Macho's body filled with one bloody hole after the next. It got to the point that I was able to stand up and Porky kept right on bussing until his guns were empty. Twenty shell casings decorated the carpet.

He looked down at Macho and spit on his bloody carcass. "All snakes gotta die muthafucka. Ain't no room in this garden for your kind." He picked up his shell casings one by one, and dropped them into the Patron bottle, kicking Macho in the ribs. "I'll have my Misfits clean up this mess. I'm sorry for the disrespectful, Homes."

Ten minutes later he had his men stuff Macho into a metal garbage can. They took his body out through the back door. Then Porky spent the next three hours completely cleaning the room with three of his men, while I sat in my office with my head on my desk. I felt depleted.

Chapter 12

I got right back to the money. Hustling as hard as I could literally two days later. In a matter of a week, I'd flown and driven across the country making drop-offs. Most times I used hustlers from my crew to do it. But it was right after, Macho got killed that I started doing it myself, and had my hittas follow close behind me. I found the peace and quiet comforting. I had so many things going through my mind that the silence was needed. The open road gave me a piece of mind and allowed me to put things into perspective. I felt like I was drowning somewhat.

I knew that I had to follow, Aaliyah's advice and get the hell out of our city, so I was finding different ways to do that in my head. I ran into Paper at Macho's burial. I was down on one knee saying a prayer in my head when he tapped me on the shoulder disrupting that.

I looked up at him with anger. "What's good, bruh?" I stood up and took his hand off me and mugged my hittas for allowing him to get so close. I would deal with them later that was for sure.

He took a step back and smiled. All his teeth looked yellow. He smelled like funk mixed with cologne. He also looked as if he was ten pounds skinnier than when I'd seen him last. "Damn, baby, it's all good." He laughed, then started to cough. He wiped his mouth with his hand. "I need some help, Rich, or should I call you Hood Rich like everybody else?"

Macho's mother walked past crying her eyes out. She shook her head and had to be held up my Macho's older sister who rubbed her back the whole way.

I walked past, Paper and stopped in front of her. "Ma'am, I'm so sorry for your loss. If there is anything I can do for you, please don't hesitate to call this number." I handed her my card and wrote my personal cell phone numbers on the back of them. I had a heavy heart. Macho was her only son.

She smiled weakly, took the card, and hugged me. "Thank you, so much, Mijo. I'll be sure to do that. God bless your clean heart." She kissed my cheek and walked away.

Porky looked on from a distance with his Ray-Ban sunglasses on. He nodded at me and put his arm around Mariella, who was breaking down beside him. Thunder roared in the sky, and I was hoping I wasn't about to get caught in the rain. Aaliyah had chosen to sit the funeral out, and I supported that. It was getting harder and harder for her to stand up. The pregnancy was getting the best of her.

Paper walked back up to me, licking his crusty white lips. They were moistened where he'd lick, but outside of that area looked as if he'd kissed a chalkboard eraser. "Say, can we talk or you gon' keep on snubbing me?"

I scoffed and looked him up and down. "Come on man, let's go and holler in my BMW. I'm parked two cars behind the hearse over there." I started to walk in that direction. My hittas closed in and I gave them a nod to let 'em know it was all good. I got to the car and popped the lock for, Paper.

He opened the door and sat in my passenger's seat. He looked all around the car in amazement. There was a constant ding sound until I closed the door on my side and started the engine with a press of a button. It purred and came to life, every television in the car flipped on to a blue screen.

Paper bucked his eyes and shook his head. "Damn, nigga, you living large ain't you?" He smiled and continued to eye the insides of my car.

I adjusted the air conditioner. "What's on your mind, Paper? Time is money." My seat began to vibrate and lightly massage my back. I angled the vent so that it blew downward. I wanted the car to be a little cooler, but I didn't want the air blowing directly on me. I moved my seat back and looked him over.

He frowned. "Damn, nigga, why you handling me like I'm one of these Peons on the street. We're supposed to be brothers."

I laughed. "Yeah, whatever happened to that?" I threw my car in drive and pulled out of that spot. I didn't know where his whip was, and I didn't care. I had to get out of that graveyard. My heart was heavy for the homie, Macho.

"Look I don't know where we fell off either, but I ain't got no time to dwell on that shit. It is what it is. So, let's turn the page." He pulled out a pack of Newports that were half gone. Popped a cigarette out of it and started to light the tip.

I rolled down the window a lil' bit on his side. I hated the smell of them. That scent mixed with the odor coming from his ass was threatening to become too much for me. "So, anyway, you saying you needed to holler at me. What's on your brain?" I looked over at him and turned the vent so that the air blew directly in my face now. I wasn't trying to catch no more whiffs of him, or that cancer stick he was smoking. I was sure I was going to get my car detailed later.

He dumped the ashes out of the window and sighed. "Nigga, I hear you're out here going hard now. Your name ringing in the streets like the bell on top of a church." He puffed off his square again and blew the smoke out of the crack of his window. The majority of it blew right back into the car, it pissed me off so bad that I wanted to punch his ass.

"So, that's what you wanted to talk about, my fame?" I sucked my teeth. "That shit don't mean nothing to me. In fact, it's more of a hindrance than anything."

"Bruh, I got fifty niggas that's up under me, and I'm down to like twenty thousand in cash. I ain't got no dope or no plug. I need you to put me on, so I can get right, and get my people right. I'm feeling like a real loser, right now." He threw the cigarette out of the window and rolled it up, then looked over at me. "So, what's up, you gon' put me on?"

"On some real shit, Paper, I shouldn't have too. Nigga, you was given the same opportunities I was. You chose to start shooting that bullshit and following your own path. Now, look at you. You look sick as a bitch." I curled my upper lip at him, looking into his yellowish, red eyes, that were glossy.

"Nigga, I don't wanna hear all that self-righteous bullshit. I'm coming at you looking for your help, not your critique. I'm tired of everybody telling me how bad I look. Or what I've done wrong. You muthafuckas don't know how it feels to lose your mother in the way that I did. That shit killed every part of me. I just never said nothing about it. Shirley offered me a way out, and I took to fucking with that pipe. It was the worst mistake of my life." He shook his head. "Did you know, Heaven, was pregnant with my shorty when I stanked her?" He blew air through his teeth. "This dope got me so fucked up that I do shit and don't regret it until the next day."

I rolled out of the graveyard, looked in my rearview mirror, and saw my hittas following behind me in the two Range Rover black on black trucks. I adjusted my seat and sat a lil' bit as I entered onto the busy intersection of Burleigh. "You fucking with that dope real heavy now. Would it be smart for me to put some of it in your hands? I mean knowing that you ain't gon' do shit wit' it, but get high?" I looked over at him and rolled through a yellow light. My Hittas made it, too and remained close behind me.

Paper pulled his nose and frowned. "So, now you gon' use that bullshit against me. What you think I don't know how to handle my bitness and keep my habit out of the equation? You think I'm that fucked up now, or something?" I could tell he was getting heated. He flared his nostrils and moved around in his seat as if he were real antsy. I knew that was a sign that he was ready to do something crazy.

I started to drive with my right hand on the steering wheel and my left I kept it rested right on the handle of my .40 Glock. Any wrong move and I was gon' fill, Paper with more holes than a golf course. "What type of work you looking for, Paper?"

He ran his tongue across his teeth. "About forty bricks of that Tar shit you flooding the hood with. I'ma hit with that fentanyl a lil' bit, just like you do, and get my numbers right. It's time I step my game all the way up. I should be balling like you are. After all, I was in the game first." He shook his head.

The clouds opened and suddenly it was bright and sunny. I rolled through the lights and got onto the highway, cruising. "Paper, what you gon' hit me with for these forty bricks? I know you don't think I'ma just drop them into your lap?"

He shrugged his shoulders. You was hitting the Misfits with product upfront and you just told them to hit you back every Friday. Why I can't get that type of treatment? You know I'm good for it if they was." He licked his crusty lips and scratched his right inner forearm.

"I don't know about no forty, Bruh. I'm fucking with some niggas that don't play about they scratch. I front you forty bricks and when it's time to pay up you wind up hitting me with a script it's gon' be done. I can't be held responsible for what happens to you. I mean that shit. Besides, why are you dead set on that number of birds? Why not some a lil' lighter?"

He slammed his fist against my dashboard. "Why you trying to stop me from handling bitness? I don't want no crumbs. I'm trying to eat like you out here eating. They should be honoring my muthafucking name, not yours. I taught you the game, remember. It was my pops putting us up on licks to help us get right. Your pink ass father wasn't nowhere in the picture. Now that he is, he put you on, and you ain't fucking wit' me. What type of shit is that, nigga?" He mugged me breathing hard.

I scrunched my face and looked him over in disgust. "Man, calm yo' ass down. Acting like you heated and shit. It ain't that I'm not trying to put yo' ass on, it's just that you come wit' so many risks because you fucking with that shit. I'm telling you, that if I hit you wit' some work and you fuck it off, Paper, I'm gon' have to knock yo' brains out on some no mercy shit. This ain't a game my nigga, and I ain't on the same level that you on."

"All you gotta do is give me a chance. I gotta qet on my shit sooner or later." He took a deep breath and exhaled slowly. "How about I drop that twenty thousand in your lap. That way it won't be like you're giving me something for nothing. I know it ain't much. But at least it's a start. What do you say?"

I pulled off the highway exit ramp and stopped at the stop sign at the top of the ramp. "I charge twenty gees a bird. That means you still gon' be seven hundred and eighty bands down. Long as you understand that we're good."

Paper pulled his nose. "I might be able to come up with a lil' more than that. But I get where you're coming from, let's make it happen." He leaned his seat back and closed his eyes.

***

The rain was back full fledge two days later. I met up with Paper at one of the furniture stores in our hood. We pulled into the back of the store damn near at the same time. I drove the delivery van for the store and had it filled with the forty kilos of heroin, and ten pounds of pure fentanyl. All in all, it was nine-hundred-thousand dollars worth of product if it sold it to somebody else in bulk. After they broke everything down and dimed it up. They were sure to make a minimum of three million in cash, that's with taking shorts. I was giving Paper the longest lifeline that I could, even though I wasn't feeling too sure about it.

He hopped out of his Escalade, just as the rain began to pour. I had two of my Hittas, carry the merch into the back of the store. I'd already decoded the system so the alarm wouldn't sound. I waved for Paper to follow me inside. Four more of my Hittas followed behind him as he made his way inside with a book bag over his right shoulder. He wore an all-black hoodie, and black jeans, over worn retro Jordan's. I made him sit on a long sofa, while I sat across from him.

There were two lamps turned on inside of the store to give us a little light to maneuver. My Hittas came and dropped the duffle bags right by my feet. I unzipped one and slapped a kilo of heroin, and one of Fentanyl onto the table, and handed him a pocket knife. I wanted him to test the product to affirm its potency.

"Be careful, that one right there is fentanyl."

He waved me off. "We better than that, Hood Rich. I trust you. The only person who ain't being trusted in this situation is me. But it's all good. I was able to come up with eighty gees. All hundreds, I know that's only four birds, but I'll get you the rest of your money. I got plans for this product, you'll see." He opened the Gucci bookbag and dug out a few stacks of money that had ten thousand dollars seals on them as if they'd come directly from a bank.

I thumbed through the bills and sniffed them. They smelled like new money. I was happy he'd come up with something. I knew, Cabo, wasn't gon' play about his bread, and for that reason, I wasn't either.

I took the book bag, and dug through it, confirming that it was filled with money. "A'ight, look, we gon' meet up every Friday just like I used to with the Misfits. You should have no less than twenty gees each time. That's the price of one bird. You handle your business and I'll handle mine. After I see that you can handle what I'm hitting you with, we'll turn up a lil' bit and really though,

I got faith in you. Just do what you gotta do." I walked around the table and gave him a hug. He smelled a lil' better and I was hoping that was a good sign. Even though, I wasn't putting too much faith in it.

We exchanged money and product, and that was that. That following Friday, instead of Paper hitting me with twenty gees, he hit me with sixty. The Friday after that he hit me with a hundred and the next one after that he hit me with two hundred gees, and I felt bad for doubting him in the first place. It didn't take long before his dressing got better. He smelled different and looked as if he had his mind right.

I still kept my distance and allowed him to do him. I didn't want us to have the type of relationship we'd once had. I was doing better being a loner and hustling under my own terms. I had to make sure I had four billion dollars sent to, Cabo every single month. So, I worked under intense pressure. Every time it was a few weeks before the deadline, I freaked out and felt like I wasn't going to make my quota. But then something would happen so that I exceeded it.

Hood Rich

Chapter 13

Aaliyah brought our daughter into the world a few months later. She came out with light caramel skin, deep dimples, freckles over her face, and a head full of wavy, curly hair. Her eyes were hazel like mine, and I was happy about that. When the doctor placed her in my arms I fell in love all over again. I was expecting her to be crying all loud and having a fit like most babies did, but she was the complete opposite. She wouldn't stop smiling with her deep dimples. She weighed six pounds, eleven ounces. I kissed her so much on the first day, that Aaliyah became jealous. I would catch her mugging me with anger.

"Dang, Rich, I get that she's your first born, but what about me. I had to spit her out. You ain't gave me a second glance since she came into the world." She rolled her eyes. I slid into the big, specially requested hospital bed with her, and put my arm around her, kissing her cheek. "Aww, now you wanna kiss on me and stuff? Yeah, okay." I could tell she wasn't playing.

She was really upset, I didn't understand it at the time, but after a while I got it. You see most women felt that after they gave a man a child he used the child to replace them in a sense, even if it was only emotionally. When more than likely, right after a woman gives birth she is at her most vulnerable. Her body is jacked up. She feels disconnected and tired. She yearns to be comforted when men are spending all our time cherishing our new baby. She didn't explain all of this to me until later, but it made sense.

I kissed her cheek, and then kissed our daughter. "I'm sorry boo, you know it ain't like that. You're still my number one. That will never change." I kissed her lips. "What are we going to name her?" I looked down at my sleeping baby girl and felt my heart doing somersaults. She was so beautiful, just like her mother. I could also see my mother, and Keyonna in her, too.

Aaliyah sat up and laid her head on my chest. It was comforting because I loved her so much already. "How about, Shante'? I've always loved that name, and she looks like a Shante' doesn't she?" She rubbed our daughter's soft cheek.

I held her in my arms and smiled. I didn't care what her first name would be. I would call her my Baby Girl, anyway. But we decided to name her Shante' and gave her Keyonna as a middle name to honor my sister. I laid in that hospital bed for the next twelve hours, holding both of my girls. There wasn't any specific reason why we didn't leave right away. But I just wanted to make sure that Aaliyah and Shante' were all good before we did.

A week after our daughter was born, Cabo sent for me. I met up with one of his underlings at Mitchell International Airport. We loaded his S-7 Private jet, and headed for Miami where I guessed, Cabo was supposed to be waiting for me. The whole time we were on that Jet, me and Cabo's underling never said a word to each other. I Facetimed Aaliyah, and Shante' as I sat in the back seat of the Jet with nothing but my family on my mind. I knew that I'd made eleven of my payments to Cabo on time, so I wasn't worried about nothing sour going down with him. I was curious as to why he wanted to see me in person, but as long as I wasn't called back to Brazil, I felt that was a good sign. I relaxed in my chair and sipped from a bottle of Patron to calm my nerves. I'd never liked flying, I had to be under some form of influence in order to be all the way up there and not freak out. I'd always been that way.

Aaliyah smiled into the phone and stuck her tongue out at me. She was without makeup, and to me, she looked finer than ever. I knew she was still a bit tired and was putting on a brave face for me. I got it, and I appreciated her for it. "Baby, when you get home we're packing and getting the hell out of here. All our properties are paid for, and all we have to do is to get to them. I'm serious, now that, Shante' is here, there is no more waiting. You got me?"

I laughed and nodded. "I got you, Boo. We out of here. I don't need more than a week. I know, I keep buying more and more time, but this time I'm serious. You've been patient and I appreciate that, Boo. I appreciate everything that you have done thus far. Especially that bundle of joy you popped out. I owe you my life for her, and I'ma dedicate the rest of it to you."

She smiled. "Aww-ah, baby. You know how emotional I am. Don't start that stuff. I can't handle it right now."

I laughed and nodded. "A'ight, Boo, I won't, but you heard what I said. After I handle this bitness, my next mission is to get our family up out of there I promise."

* * *

We arrived in Miami, at nine p.m., Cabo and two of his security guards met us in the tangar. We stepped out of the Jet and got into a stretch Mercedes Benz limousine. When I climbed into the back of the limo the first thing I felt was the air conditioner blowing into my face. Cabo sat in the back smoking on a fat cigar, blowing big clouds of smoke, with a smile on his face.

"Hood Rich, mi companero', come on in and have a seat." He pointed at the couch across from him.

There were already two security men with cowboy hats seated on it. There was a space in between them that I guessed was for me, so, I took it. Cabo opened a box of Cuban cigars and directed me to grab one out, but I declined. Tobacco ain't do nothing but give me a headache. I wasn't wit' that at all. He put the box away, and handed me a bottle of Hornitos, pulling the cap off first.

"Then have a sip of this. It's from the heart of my land. You'll love it." He blew out a cloud of smoke, holding the cigar with his teeth. His big bushy mustache was curled at the ends. He looked like Old Sammy Sam from the cartoons, with black hair.   I took a sip from the bottle and handed it back to him. He set it on the table beside him and sat back. "Hood Rich," he laughed. "There is no need to be alarmed. I just wanted to check in with you and let you know that you are doing a great job. All the cities I've put you in control of are getting their dope on time. My funds are adding up the right way. It's a well-oiled machine. It's time to lock you in for life." He laughed and puffed on his cigar some more.

Smoke wafted into the air and made my stomach turn. I hated that shit. I scrunched my face. "Wait, what are you talking about locking me in for life?" I was confused and needed clarification, so, I could know what I was up against. I knew he was a trickster.

He leaned forward. "Well, now, that I know you're a man I can depend on, I'm choosing to depend on you until your last breath. It means that right now, until your heart stops you are my slave. You've made more than enough money. You'll never be able to pay me back in the short time that you are alive, so instead of trying, you'll just work until I'm done with you. It's simple of that." He took the bottle of Hornitos from the table and threw it out the window. It shattered in the street. "I don't drink behind my peasants." He had a scowl on his face that rubbed me the wrong way. I wish I could have blown his brains out, I didn't like this man.

I mugged him and felt my heart pounding in my chest. "I ain't nobody's slave. If I don't wanna fuck with you no more, then that'll just be that. Fuck what you talking about."

Cabo laughed, and so did his men on the side of me. He pointed at me as if I'd cracked a joke. He laughed so hard that tears came out of his eyes. He slapped his thigh, and his face turned a shade pinkish red. "You hear this, Vato? He sounds all tough and shit. *If I don't want to work anymore it's just going to be that. I'm nobody's slave.*" He busted out laughing again. "Fucking Cavron!"

"What the fuck is so funny?" I was ready to jump across the aisle and attack his ass. I knew his men would probably kill me, but I was so mad, I didn't even care. I didn't like how he was trying to treat me like a bitch. I would rather die a gangsta than a bitch any day.

Cabo dabbed at his tears with a cloth and turned his face into a deadly scowl. "You see, that's where you got it all wrong. You're going to work for me until I say you're done. You owe me four million dollars every single month, and come hell or high water, if you're alive, you're going to pay it. Or your daughter will be fed to my pig after I slice Aaliyah's in front of you. You don't understand who you're fucking with but sit back, because you will in a minute," he spat.

He wiped his nose with his hand and sniffed loudly. I sat back in the couch fuming. I was so hot that I felt killing him and his guards, but I knew I stood no chance at that. I was in Miami, with no security, and no pistols. Just like in Brazil, I was completely at his mercy. I feared what he was about to show me. I didn't fear him, just the things he was capable of. I couldn't believe he'd actually said something about Shante', she was just a newborn, and not even a month old at this point.

About an hour later, we pulled into a shrimp packaging plant, right off the Port. The moonlight shined off the water, as it rippled northward. The Limo pulled around to the back of the place. I could hear the gravel under the tires. When we rolled up, we were met by five armed men who were just getting off a boat that was docked in the back of the plant. They wore Cowboy hats, like Cabo, beside their boat was two other ones, attached to the back of them were big nets that were rolled up. It smelled like fish and seaweed. There was strong stench of piss as well. I looked out if the windows and watched the armed guards come and aim their weapons at the back doors where we would eventually exit.

"After you see what I got in there for you, Hood Rich. You're going to do everything I say without giving me any talkback. It's amazing I haven't put a bullet in that nugget of yours already." He frowned, as the door opened. "Let's go."

I was led into the back of the plant with an assault Rifle poking in my back. It wasn't really necessary, because I wasn't trying to go nowhere. I was stuck. His comments of what he'd do to my girls were heavy on my mind. I needed to find a way to kill this sick son of a bitch. We stepped inside of the plant, it looked like a big warehouse on the inside. It was full of brown wooden crates that were filled with shrimp, and salmon. It smelled horrible like a whale's ass, or what I would imagine a whale's ass to smell like. It was hot and humid, the air was thick, and it made it hard to breathe. I could taste the salt in the atmosphere as well, and that was odd to me.

I was ushered through a bunch of crates. They were lined up as if they were sorted in a certain way. We passed more than one Forklift, big rats crawled around on the floor in twos. Cabo walked up ahead along with the man that I'd flown on the private Jet with. They spoke in Spanish and I was only able to make out a few words, not enough to make sense of anything. After traveling for five minutes, we made it to the other side of the plant. We walked through a big metal door, and into a well-lit room. As soon as we walked through it my mouth dropped wide open. There was a big oak table in the middle of the room with chairs all around it. At the head of the table was my father. Two of, Cabo's men stood behind him with assault rifles pointed against the back of his head. He looked red and worn out, I began to panic right away.

"Son, what are you doing here?"

I was slammed into a seat one chair over from him. Cabo sat at the foot of the table and ordered the other men to do the same. "Everybody have a seat." He cracked his knuckles and took his hat off his head. He was balding in the middle, his long, stringy hair stopped at the center of his head. There was a pink circle there, a circle that he scratched. "Go ahead, exchange your pleasantries, then let's get on with the fucking business. I don't have all day, Cavrons."

My father turned to me and swallowed. "I'm sorry, I got you roped into this, Rich. Please know that I love you."

Now I was really panicking because I didn't understand what was going on. I didn't like the look of fear in my father's eyes. I didn't understand how my father could have been so plugged in the Mafia, but Cabo easily kept him under the gun. I was beginning to understand that whoever ran the drug trade in North America, was the one that ran the world. My father seemed to be nothing more than a rodent when it came to, Cabo.

Cabo sighed. "Okay, it seems that you fucked me out of my Vegas and Atlantic city deal, Paulie, it turns out, you don't have as much power within the Bertolli family as you thought, in fact, they're promising to give me the same deal that you offered if I cut your fucking head off. Now that's a turn of events."

I almost broke my neck turning to my father. He had his head down in defeat, he was flushed and looked weak and sick. I felt horrible for him.

Cabo stood up. "The thing is, this Cavron right here has already been working under me long enough to score a few million dollars in his own right. He's connected to a cartel of animals that wiped out my nephew's crew that were stationed in Milwaukee, and I let it slide, only because you promised me red carpet treatment in Vegas, and Atlantic City. Now that I know you can't deliver, one of you are not leaving this room alive. It's either you're going to die, or," he sighed. "Or your son." He laughed. "I still find that fucking hilarious. I'll give you two a moment to decide." He pulled out a cigar and lit the tip, took his seat, and crossed one leg over the other. His Snake skinned boats shined in the room.

"Neither one of us needs to die, Cabo. I can fix this. You have to give me a chance, too. I'm still connected, trust me."

Cabo slammed his hand on the table. "Shut up you fucking idiot! The Bertolli family knows you are the one that set up the Don. Your sins have caught up with you. Whether I kill you or not, they're going too. It's best that you make it easier on yourself and let your son live. He has his whole life ahead of him. You're finished," he snapped.

My father shook his head. "That's nonsense, I have obligations. He's just a kid. If he dies nobody will give a shit. Me, I'm important. If it comes down to who lives and who dies, then I choose me." He frowned and looked across the table at Cabo with anger. He balled his fist until the knuckles were white.

I bucked my eyes and felt my heart tear into two. My nose felt like I'd sniffed an onion. My eyes watered, and a tear dropped out of them. I couldn't believe my father my own flesh and blood, had said that I was hurt.

Cabo sucked his tongue to the top of his mouth and made a loud clicking sound repeatedly while shaking his head. "You're a dirty son of a bitch aren't you, Paulie? You throw your own son under the bus as if he's nothing. Maybe it's because of his skin, huh, Paulie?" Cabo laughed.

My father shook his head. "It has nothing to do with his skin complexion. It's about what I can bring to the table and what he can't. He's just a street dealer, sooner or later he'll be gunned down by a rival gang, or something worst that takes place in the hood. If you put your eggs in his basket they are guaranteed to be crushed and found useless. I am a man, of many connections, I can

offer you ten times more than he can, and you know it,"
He spat, with saliva flying out of his mouth.

I was looking him over in disbelief. My head shook
from side to side. I was stunned. My own father doing to
me what I would never do to a son or my daughter.

"You hear this shit, Hood Rich? This is the father that
you've been cursed with. It sucks, doesn't it? This man is
so easy to throw you to the wolves to be killed and rav-
ished." He leaned over my chair and placed his cheek
against mine. "What do you have to say for yourself,
Hood Rich?"

I looked at my old man and wiped my tears away. I'd
already lost my mother, by my own doing. Dropped the
ball when it came to my sister, Keyonna. Now I was faced
with a decision that would keep my father alive or kill
him. I was stuck, I felt angry and sick to my stomach at
the same time. I questioned life altogether. Why had I
been placed here? Why had all those I truly cared for died
with me having something to do with it? I just didn't understand.

"Pop, so you'd be cool with them killing me, right
now?" I asked.

He looked at me and scrunched his face. "It ain't
nothing personal son, it's just business. It's like in the Bi-
ble, had David, allowed his army to kill Absalom a long
time ago, it would have saved him a world of pain and
strife. So yes."

I lowered my head and shook it. "Damn, you had to
say that."

Cabo patted me on the back and snapped his fingers.
One of his security men handed him a machete. Cabo
walked back to his seat and stood in front of it.

"I am a man that loves power and money. In that order. Now the Bertolli and Battaglia family has made me an offer that I can't refuse. Your head is worth millions to me, Paulie. And I will be given the same power that you offered, along with the Port of Florida. Am I to past up this opportunity, because you are making me promises that you are pulling out of your ass? Then, if you'd do this to your son, I can only imagine what type of businessman, you'd be down the line. No thank you."

"On the other hand, Rich, you have a snake's DNA. That scares me, and very little scares, old Cabo. To kill a snake, you must cut off its head. For you to go back to your life, under my care, you must walk around this table. Take this machete and cut your father's head off his body and set it right here." His security man handed him a silver platter. He slammed it onto the long table in front of him. He held the machete out to me. "Do you hear me?"

I lowered my head and shook it. Images of Shante' and Aaliyah popped up in my head. Then came my mother, followed by Keyonna, and Kesha. I felt even sicker than I had before. I didn't think I could kill my old man. He was my father, the only parent I had left.

"Cabo, don't do this, give the machete to me. I'll kill him with no hesitation. He's nothing, let me at 'em," my father spat all over the table. He tried to get up, and the security men behind him slammed him back into his seat aggressively.

Cabo slammed the machete on the table again. This time so hard that it echoed in my ears. I jumped and got angry. "What are you going to do, Hood Rich? Either him, or you. Keep in mind that if you die, then so does your daughter and her mother. I have men parked two houses down from your place in West Allis as we speak.

One word and they will dismember the two of them with no mercy or care for them. You three will meet in Heaven." He laughed. "Tell me what it is, now!"

More images of my daughter and Aaliyah filled my brain. So much so that my nose started to bleed. It ran past my lips, and over my chin. I felt dizzy as I imagined the Mexicans hurting my girls. I couldn't allow that to happen. I was their protector. I'd been placed on earth to make sure that no harm ever came to them. I couldn't drop the ball again. I just couldn't.

"Give it to me, Cabo. I understand the game, give it to me. We'll work this out. I will not fail, you again, I swear it," my father shouted rising from his seat again. There was a thick vein in the side of his neck. Sweat ran down the side of his face and he mugged me with hatred.

I took the machete from Cabo and scooted my chair from under me. My eyes were misty. No matter how much dumb shit he was talking, he was still my father. My flesh and blood, I would never be able to get over what I was about to do to him for as long as I lived.

His eyes lowered into slits. "You don't have the guts son. You're a pussy. You get your heart from your mother's side of the family. Not mine!"

Cabo snapped his fingers and both guards that were standing behind my father forced his face into the table. Cabo slid the platter to them. My father struggled to break their holds, but they were stronger and more determined to follow Cabo's orders than meeting death themselves.

Cabo stood up. "Hold that Cavron steady! Let his son cut his head off like he deserves. Go ahead, Hood Rich, you do this and you're square with me. It takes cohonas, Vato." He balled his fingers into fists and held it in the air.

I walked beside my father and took a deep breath, clutching the Machete tight in my right hand. "You got any last words?"

He grunted. "Make sure you take it clean off with one slash." He spit toward me and missed. "I hope you rot in hell you, filthy turn coat. Send my best to, Kesha. Let's go!"

I raised it over my head, and Cabo's men leaned back enough to get out of the way, but they kept a firm grasp on my father. I tried to imagine all the times he'd beaten my mother when I was a kid. How he'd gotten her addicted to heroin before we moved from out east. How he'd neglected our family for his own pure Italian bred one. Even with all these things going through my head, I was still unable to go through with killing him. Something in me just wouldn't allow myself too.

Cabo took his phone out of his pocket, dialed something on it, and held up a picture of me pushing Aaliyah out of the hospital in a wheelchair, while she held our bundle of joy.

"You got five seconds to kill that filthy snake before I have them, and you executed. He'll go on with his life and never think about you again. He's dirty like that."

"Fuck you, Rich! I hope he kills you and that fucking kid! You're a pussy. A peasant, weak, just like your mother!" My father snapped with spit flying from his mouth.

Cabo walked over and grabbed a handful of his hair. "Do it, Hood Rich. Do it, now," he ordered. "Five seconds!"

I raised the machete higher, as my father continued to swear under me. Imagined how Shante' looked coming out of Aaliyah's womb, then imagined somebody doing something to hurt either one of my girls. I clenched my teeth, and brought the machete down with all my might, severing his head from his body.

Chapter 14

I got home two days later. When I pulled up there were two black Mercedes Benz cars parked in my driveway. They had Texas plates and dark tinted windows. I slammed the door to my Uber, paid the man and ran full speed to my front door. Aaliyah had not been answering the phone this entire day and that caused me to grow worried about her, and Shante'. I took my key and jiggled it into the lock. Before I could push it in, it opened, and I was pulled inside by a big Italian bodyguard that looked like he played in the NFL. He was huge and smelled like Old Spice cologne.

He pointed a .9 millimeter in my face and frowned. "Hood Rich?" He asked, closing the door behind us.

"Where the fuck is my woman and kid?" I hollered, getting ready to panic. I looked over his shoulder toward the back of the house, feeling like I was about to throw up all over the floor.

"Rich-Rich!" Aaliyah yelled and ran into the front room from the back of the house. She ran and wrapped her arms around me.

"Baby, what's the matter?" I kissed her forehead and held in her front of me. "Where is Shante'?"

Another tall Italian walked into the room bouncing a sleeping, Shante' up and down in his arms. He cooed to her and smiled at us. "Paulie's been taken care of, lucky for you and your family, Rich. You took care of business in just a nick of time."

He handed Shante' to me and bumped me as he walked past. Your sins are forgiven. You have a nice life. You're Cabo's bitch."

Six other men walked out of the house behind him and the big NFL looking guard. As soon as the door was closed, Aaliyah dropped to her knees with her hands covering her face. She broke into a fit of tears, sobbing loudly. "I can't take this shit no more, Rich. I just can't. You promised me that we would be out of here already. We're still here. Now there are people forcing their way into our home in the middle of the night. Ripping, Shante' out of my arms, and won't even let me change her diapers. And I won't even mention what they did to me when they so-called searched me for weapons. Thankfully, I just had her, and the stitches are still in or we would have been in trouble." She shook her head and lowered her face to the carpet.

All of her crying woke, Shante' out of her slumber. She opened her little eyes, stretched her arms above her head, and yawned.

I bounced her up and down. "Baby, go pack our things. We're getting the hell out of here, first thing in the morning. Do you hear me, Lil' One?" I grabbed her arm and pulled her to her feet.

I noted that she had hickeys all over her neck. This got me angry. I wanted to kill the Italians that I assumed were from the Bertolli family. I felt like once again I had put someone, I truly loved under the gun by the poor decisions that I had made. Aaliyah was my Lil' One, my everything. Just imagining another man even touching her was enough to make me wanna go ballistic. I hugged her tighter to me.

She shook her head. "Screw that, Rich. I'm taking our daughter, and I'm getting out of here tonight. I don't care about nothing that is left behind in this house. We can get it again. We have more than enough money to do so. I am begging you to come with us. You can handle everything else that you need too over the phone." She looked into my eyes, searchingly.

I handed her, Shante' and shook my head. "That's cool baby, you go ahead and do what you have, too. Why don't you take our daughter to a hotel or something for the night? Book us two one-way First-Class tickets to Houston, and I'll meet you at the Hotel the first thing in the morning. No later than ten you got my word on that, Boo."

She sighed and lowered her head, then looked up at me. "Okay, but you better stand on your word. We're leaving all of this behind as of tomorrow. Please keep that promise, Rich. Our lives depend on it." She kissed my lips and took Shante' to the back of the house where they began getting ready.

* * *

I met up with, Chasity an hour later. She was in her office at our downtown club going over payrolls on her laptop. When she saw me, she jumped up and ran around the desk, wrapped her arms around my neck and kissed my lips. "Hey baby, where have you been? Why you ain't answering none of your phones? I've been worried sick over you." She slapped me on the chest and walked back around the desk, sitting down.

She put her Chanel eyeglasses on her face. They made her look like a sophisticated, strapped ass model. She popped her shiny lips and waited for my response. Her tongue dabbed at the corner of her mouth.

"Look, I'm about to take a trip for a few months. I'ma leave you in charge of our clubs up here. I feel like you can handle it. You been doing a good job so far." I moved the big fish tank out of the way by rolling it. It was against the wall in her office. After moving it, I pushed on the wall twice and it popped open. I pulled the latch and exposed our big safe inside of it. I keyed in the digital combination, and it popped open. "How much bread we got in here, right now?"

Chasity hopped out of her seat, came behind me and wrapped her arms around my waist, then laid her head on my back. "It's two point six million in this one. And three even in the one on North Avenue. Why, are you looking to take some of it with you? And where the fuck are you going anyway?" She stepped to the side, looking me over very closely. "Are you in some sort of trouble? Don't lie either."

I shook my head. "Naw, Aaliyah, just need a change in scenery. So, I'ma give her what she asking for. She been stomp down since day one. She deserves to be happy." I grabbed her Gucci bag and turned it upside down on her desk. Spilling out all the contents. They crashed on top of her desk loudly.

"Hey! That's a lil' rude ain't it? You could of asked me first."

I scoffed and loaded seven hundred thousand dollars into the Gucci bag, stuffing it to the max, before zipping it up. "All the rest of this paper is for you to keep the clubs running smoothly. I ain't gon' touch none of it from North Avenue. That's all you. You always said that this has been your dream. To own your own business, well here you go. I'ma make sure security stay in place, but I would like for you to orchestrate your own body of security as well."

"Rich, why you acting like you can't answer none of my questions? I know you hear me asking them?" She rolled her eyes.

I tighten my grip on the Gucci bag and smiled down at her. "I done got enough people hurt in my time, Chasity. I feel like the less you know the better." I pulled her to me and kissed her cheeks. "I want you to know that I cared about you, a lot. I always will. Anything you need I will only be a phone call away. I trust you to handle your business. Don't allow nothing or nobody to stand in your way of success. You've lost enough in your life. It's time to turn the page."

She hugged me with all her might. "So, you just gon' leave me then, Rich. You helped me build all of this, then you just gon' run off with her? Even though, you know, I need you just as much?" She blinked, and tears fell down her cheeks. She looked up at me and pulled on my shirt. "Take me with you. I ain't trying to break up your happy home. But something tells me that you aren't coming back. So, take me too, please."

I dropped the bag, and wrapped her into my arms, holding her for a moment, feeling like I was betraying, Aaliyah and Shante' in the process. I broke our embrace and brushed her curls out of her face. "Chasity, you're good, ma. You don't need me or no other man in order to make things happen for yourself. I'm giving you two strip clubs when you only wanted us to open one. You're financially stable. You got your own home, that's bought and paid for. Two whips, and a Range Rover. You're a healthy, stable of women, what more can you ask for?"

She shook her head. "I know, Rich, but none of this shit means anything if I ain't got you to share it with. I wouldn't have none of it if it wasn't for you. I owe you my loyalty and my life. How can I give either of them to you if you aren't even around?" She scrunched her face and tears dripped out of her eyes. She sniffed snot back into her nose and began to sob.

I held her firmer and exhaled. "You got this, ma. You're a champion. You as strong as any man. Keep your goals at the forefront of your mind. Stand on them women and make them pay the way for you. Be fair and stay in prayer. You'll be good."

She continued to break down for a full ten minutes while I rubbed her back. When she finally calmed down, she took a deep breath and blew it out, slowly. She looked into my hazel eyes and swallowed.

"Rich, I ain't never met a man like you before, and I know I probably never will again. I hope I see you again. But if I don't, I want you to know that I love you. I have always been in love with you ever since we were kids. And I thank the Lord above for bringing you into my life. I'ma handle my business and never hit bottom again. I promise this to you. Now gimme a hug." She hugged me close and cried into my chest some more. "I wish we would have made a baby together or something. How about we get together one more time for old time's sake. I'll let you do anything you want to me. Long as you come in me, and not on me." She looked into my eyes, serious.

I started imagining all the times we'd been together and how good they were. I thought about her moans, and how it felt to go deep into her thick ass body. She had a real ghetto booty that shook every time I crashed into it from the back. Her head game was on point, and all in all she was a good fuck. But then, Aaliyah and Shante's face popped into my mind. I owed the both more loyalty and respect than that. I had to be a man and raise my family.

I'd hurt them enough. I exhaled loudly and looked down on, Chasity. She ran her pink tongue over her juicy lips and grabbed my pipe through my pants.

I caught her wrist and took it away from me. "Naw, ma, I know it'll be fun, but I can't get down like that no more."

She lowered her head. "Dang, I wish you loved me like that." She hugged me again, and broke down for the last time, before I kissed her cheeks, and left her in the office sitting behind the desk with her head on top of it.

* * *

Porky gave me a half of hug and patted my back. I sat down across from him in the living room of his tuck away crib that he shared with his baby mother and two sons. Since the death of Macho, he'd made, Mariella move in as well. When their mother found out she was pregnant she'd nearly beaten the baby right out of her. Under normal circumstances, Porky would have allowed it, but since she was carrying, Macho's baby, he hadn't. There was a big smart screen television hanging on the wall of the basement. He had it on ESPN. The world was waiting to see where LeBron was headed after opting out of his contract with Cleveland. They'd just been swept in the NBA Finals by the Golden State Warriors.

Porky muted the television and smiled at me. He picked up a blunt from the table and tried to hand it to me, but I declined. He didn't have a shirt on. I saw that he had a fresh tat of Macho's face on his chest. It read, *R.I.P. My Brother*.

"How you been, lil' homie?" I sat back on the couch, and relaxed.

He shook his head and sighed. "I been fucked up. I should have never killed him, Hood Rich. Ain't nothing the same no more." He sparked the blunt and inhaled the smoke into his lungs. "I see him in my dreams too. All he keeps asking me is why I did it?" How could I kill him? I hear it so vividly." He winced and put the blunt into the ashtray. Took out two Percocet pills and chewed them up. Then chased them with swallows from the Patron that was on the table. He wiped sweat from his brow.

"I'm getting out of here, lil' Homie. I gotta have a fresh start, I owe that to my Lil' One, and my daughter."

Porky sucked his teeth and closed his eyes. "I don't blame you, Homes." He picked up the bottle of Patron and turned it up. "Ain't nothing but heartache and pain here, Ese. I should think about the same thing, but Macho's spirit haunts me wherever I go. I'm trapped, Homes." He shook his head from right to left and drank more of the liquor, guzzling greedily.

I nodded in understanding. "I got a few spirits that haunt me as well. It's part of the game, gotta take along with the territory. I just wanted you to know that I was leaving. I never held what you did to the homie against you. You're my brother and I love you, kid." I leaned over the table and pulled him up. We embraced, and I patted his back. "Be strong, man, Macho, will let you rest sooner or later. You feel me?"

Porky nodded and shook his head. "I love you, too, big bruh. You've always been one hunnit to me and him. Because of you, The Misfits are now an Army grossing a million dollars every two weeks. I can't repay you for that." He lowered his head. "I wish Macho, was here man. I fucked up." He crumbled to the couch and whimpered deep within his throat.

I consoled him as much as I could for the next hour. Then I left to meet up with, Paper. Two weeks after this day, Porky committed suicide in Mariella's bedroom right after confessing that he'd been the one that killed, Macho. He blew his head off right in front of her, with a sawed-off shotgun. When I got the news, I was devastated, but I understood.

* * *

I met Paper at the old aluminum recycling plant on thirtieth and Auer Avenue. Chasity had told him that I was leaving, and he'd said that he wanted to cop thirty bricks of heroin from me before I did. He was also supposed to have the remaining five hundred grand he owed. I had fifty kilos left on me at this time. I decided that I would kill two birds with one stone. I'd get the money, Paper owed me, and give him the remaining kilos, and make sure he'd have the information where to send my money digitally from now on. In my own mind, he'd gotten better. I felt that he was finally in a position where I could trust him to do the right thing. His traps were flourishing. He was coming up with large sums of money in record time, so whatever he was doing had to be working. I felt I was making the right decision. After all he'd been my right and ever since we were kids in elementary school. I owed him this. At least it was how I felt.

He pulled up in a red Lexus truck, banging out of control. The truck had gold Sprewells on them, and the paint was candy coated. He hopped out, walked around to the driver's side of my BMW, and gave me a hug. "Damn, nigga, I guess its finally time for you to move on, huh?" He hugged me tighter and sighed.

I nodded. "It's time to do some grown-up things, bruh. But before I leave, I'm giving you the game. I got fifty bricks in the truck. Give me fifteen a piece, here go the information to send everything to me from here on out. I'ma come through this way every other month to see what's good. But other than that, it's all yours, Paper." Even in the night, I could see his eyes light up. I hugged him again and popped my trunk.

We broke our embrace. He snatched a black duffle bag from his truck and set it on the hood of my BMW. He unzipped it and pulled out a stack of ten thousand. "It's a million even in this bag, bruh. Once I get all the way right, I'll have the rest for you. I appreciate everything. Know that I'd never do anything unless I was forced, too. I love you, dawg." He slid the money across the hood of the car.

I caught it and looked inside, everything looked Kosher to me. I took it and tossed it onto the floor of my back seat, and gave, Paper the two Louis Vuitton suitcases filled with heroin.

He opened one and looked inside, then held up a silver package, and laughed out loud. "Hell yeah, this that heat too. I appreciate it, Boss. I'll never forget this." He hugged me again. "Take care of yourself, I'll see you soon." He patted my back and got into his truck after loading the suitcases inside.

I walked around to my driver's side and began to back out of the parking lot. I'd already hit Aaliyah's cell to let her know, I was on my way to the Hotel, we would be leaving the first thing in the morning. Our flight was scheduled to leave at eleven-fifteen. I couldn't wait to start over, even though I knew that, Cabo was going to be a problem for the future. I didn't know how I was going to handle him yet, but I would figure it out.

Paper hit his horn three times, then stormed out of the lot ahead of me. I watched his brake lights come on, and then they went off. He stormed away, as soon as he turned the corner what seemed like fifty Black SUVs came out of everywhere with sirens on their dashboard. They boxed me in from all angles, jumped out of their trucks, with assault rifles in their hands aimed at me. I had so many weapons pointed at me that if I had moved an inch I would have been slain.

Hood Rich

Chapter 15

I sat at the defendant's table with my head down a month later, while Paper sat on the stand and pointed me out in front of a grand jury. He'd told them everything that we'd done together, and even some of the things that we hadn't. I sat there heated, while he went on and on. He'd even blamed, Heaven's murder on me. Aaliyah sat behind me crying her eyes out. Her face was bright red. She looked as if she'd lost about twenty pounds. Her hair looked thinner, there were dark circles under her eyes as well. I felt sick to my stomach. Shante' bounced up and down in her arms, smiling. Her deep dimples were on full display. She didn't have a care in the world, I imagined. I missed her so much.

Kesha had flown in for the date. Her face was so covered in tears. She shook her head as Paper painted the most horrible picture he could of me. When he finished, the Grand Jury had chosen to indict, and the State was laying in the weeds, so they could charge me with the multiple murders. Paper had found all the dead bodies and bodies and dug them up for them. They'd given him full immunity. So, he could say and show them anything and they wouldn't do a damn thing about it. I just knew I was fucked.

Cabo wasn't the type of man to take a loss. He felt like he owned me and had sent word through his team of attorneys that he was going to get me off, and I would be forced to repay him when I got out. He flew in two of the top attorneys from Los Angeles, and two from Boston. They, in turn, assembled a legal team that dismantled every allegation Paper had brought before the grand jury. I was able to beat all of them, except for the deliveries of heroin, I'd made to him. He'd been working with the feds all alone. They had the bricks, and the marked money to go against me as evidence. When it was all said and done, Cabo pulled some strings, and I walked away with a hundred and twenty months. I was being told I would only have to serve eighty-five percent of it, which was more than cool with me. I was just thankful to have my life back.

Four months after I was sentenced, they found Paper beheaded in his living room. His head had been placed on a silver platter and a big rat was stuffed into his mouth.

Shawn looked up at me with her right eyebrow raised. She had flown all the way to Wisconsin to see me after I'd been sentenced.

"Damn, all of this happened in that short period of time." She shook her head. "You done been through a lot, do you want to put any of this in your books?"

Kesha reached across the table and grabbed my hand. "My brother ain't never been one to sugar coat nothing. He gone give it to his readers just like it came to him. Ain't that right, big bro?"

Shawn sucked on her bottom lip and nodded her head. "Well, if that's the case, then that's how it's gon' go. We're here to support you. For as long as you're *locked down*, you won't ever have to worry about anything." She went over financial and other particulars and then asked, "That sounds good to you?"

I nodded. "I can't do nothing but keep it real. Every book I drop with your company gotta be uncut, or I don't want y'all putting it out. This is my legacy."

She slid the contract across the table and looked up at me. I nodded and signed on the dotted line. "Expect nothing but the real from me. Send my love to the homie, Ca$h."

* * *

This is only the third of twelve books I got for the world. I sit back and reminisce about all the things that I've seen and been through, and it's like my pen can't write fast enough. Aaliyah, still holding me down stronger than ever. She turned the real state game upside down in Texas. She and I are married now and tear that ass up twice a month on our conjugal visits. She's becoming a stronger, more secure woman, and I love her with all my heart. She's stomp down and when I touch down in a few years, she'll never have to work again.

Cabo is still lying in the weeds and awaiting my release. I'm in the rear four million a month no matter what. I don't know how things are going to shake with him when I to touch down, but I was thankful for him saving my life.

I pledge allegiance to the Trap, Hood Rich.

The End

Submission Guideline.

Submit the first three chapters of your completed manuscript to ldpsubmissions@gmail.com, subject line: Your book's title. The manuscript must be in a .doc file and sent as an attachment. Document should be in Times New Roman, double spaced and in size 12 font. Also, provide your synopsis and full contact information. If sending multiple submissions, they must each be in a separate email.

Have a story but no way to send it electronically? You can still submit to LDP/Ca$h Presents. Send in the first three chapters, written or typed, of your completed manuscript to:

LDP: Submissions Dept
Po Box 870494
Mesquite, Tx 75187

DO NOT send original manuscript. Must be a duplicate.

Provide your synopsis and a cover letter containing your full contact information.

Thanks for considering LDP and Ca$h Presents.

BOW DOWN TO MY GANGSTA

By **Ca$h**

TORN BETWEEN TWO

By **Coffee**

BLOOD STAINS OF A SHOTTA **III**

By **Jamaica**

STEADY MOBBIN II

By **Marcellus Allen**

BLOOD OF A BOSS **V**

By **Askari**

LOYAL TO THE GAME **IV**

By **T.J. & Jelissa**

A DOPEBOY'S PRAYER **II**

By **Eddie "Wolf" Lee**

IF LOVING YOU IS WRONG… **III**

LOVE ME EVEN WHEN IT HURTS

By **Jelissa**

TRUE SAVAGE **V**

By **Chris Green**

BLAST FOR ME **III**

ROTTEN TO THE CORE **III**

By **Ghost**

ADDICTIED TO THE DRAMA **III**

By **Jamila Mathis**

LIPSTICK KILLAH **III**

CRIME OF PASSION **II**

By **Mimi**

WHAT BAD BITCHES DO **III**

By **Aryanna**

THE COST OF LOYALTY **II**

By **Kweli**

SHE FELL IN LOVE WITH A REAL ONE **II**

By **Tamara Butler**

LOVE SHOULDN'T HURT **III**

By **Meesha**

CORRUPTED BY A GANGSTA **III**

By **Destiny Skai**

A GANGSTER'S CODE III

By **J-Blunt**

KING OF NEW YORK II

By **T.J. Edwards**

CUM FOR ME **IV**

By **Ca$h & Company**

Available Now

RESTRAINING ORDER **I & II**

By **CA$H & Coffee**

LOVE KNOWS NO BOUNDARIES **I II & III**

By **Coffee**

RAISED AS A GOON I, II, III & IV

BRED BY THE SLUMS I, II, III

BLAST FOR ME I & II

ROTTEN TO THE CORE I II

By **Ghost**

LAY IT DOWN **I & II**

LAST OF A DYING BREED

BLOOD STAINS OF A SHOTTA I & II

By **Jamaica**

LOYAL TO THE GAME

LOYAL TO THE GAME II

LOYAL TO THE GAME III

By **TJ & Jelissa**

BLOODY COMMAS I & II

SKI MASK CARTEL I II & III

KING OF NEW YORK

By **T.J. Edwards**

IF LOVING HIM IS WRONG…I & II

By **Jelissa**

WHEN THE STREETS CLAP BACK I & II III

By **Jibril Williams**

A DISTINGUISHED THUG STOLE MY HEART I II & III

LOVE SHOULDN'T HURT I II

By **Meesha**

A GANGSTER'S CODE I & II

By J-Blunt

PUSH IT TO THE LIMIT

By **Bre' Hayes**

BLOOD OF A BOSS **I, II, III & IV**

Hood Rich

By **Askari**

By **Jerry Jackson**

An **LDP Erotica Collaboration**

By **Destiny Skai**

By **Adrienne**

By **Aryanna**

I MURDER FOR THE DOUGH

By **Ambitious**

TRUE SAVAGE

TRUE SAVAGE II

TRUE SAVAGE **III**

TRUE SAVAGE **IV**

By **Chris Green**

A DOPEBOY'S PRAYER

By **Eddie "Wolf" Lee**

THE KING CARTEL **I, II & III**

By **Frank Gresham**

THESE NIGGAS AIN'T LOYAL **I, II & III**

By **Nikki Tee**

GANGSTA SHYT **I II &III**

By **CATO**

THE ULTIMATE BETRAYAL

By **Phoenix**

BOSS'N UP **I , II & III**

By **Royal Nicole**

I LOVE YOU TO DEATH

By Destiny J

I RIDE FOR MY HITTA

I STILL RIDE FOR MY HITTA

By **Misty Holt**

LOVE & CHASIN' PAPER

By **Qay Crockett**

TO DIE IN VAIN

Hood Rich

By **ASAD**

BROOKLYN HUSTLAZ

By **Boogsy Morina**

BROOKLYN ON LOCK I & II

By **Sonovia**

GANGSTA CITY

By **Teddy Duke**

A DRUG KING AND HIS DIAMOND I & II

A DOPEMAN'S RICHES

By **Nicole Goosby**

TRAPHOUSE KING I II & III

By **Hood Rich**

LIPSTICK KILLAH **I, II**

CRIME OF PASSION

By **Mimi**

STEADY MOBBN'

By **Marcellus Allen**

BOOKS BY LDP'S CEO, CA$H

TRUST IN NO MAN

TRUST IN NO MAN 2

TRUST IN NO MAN 3

BONDED BY BLOOD

SHORTY GOT A THUG

THUGS CRY

THUGS CRY 2

THUGS CRY 3

TRUST NO BITCH

TRUST NO BITCH 2

TRUST NO BITCH 3

TIL MY CASKET DROPS

RESTRAINING ORDER

RESTRAINING ORDER 2

IN LOVE WITH A CONVICT

Coming Soon

BONDED BY BLOOD 2

BOW DOWN TO MY GANGSTA

Hood Rich